KANOKO OKAMOTO

The Tale of an Old Geisha
AND OTHER STORIES

CAPRA PRESS
1985

Gratitude to the National Endowment for the Arts
for their valuable assistance.

Library of Congress Cataloging in Publication Data
Main entry under title:
THE WHITE BLACKBIRD (The Capra back-to-back series)
I. Nin, Anaïs, 1903-1977. White blackbird. 1985.
II. Okamoto, Kanoko, 1889-1939. Rogi sho. English. 1985.
PS3527.I865W46   1985   813'.52   84-21465
ISBN 0-88496-229-6 (pbk.)

PUBLISHED BY
CAPRA PRESS
Post Office Box 2068
Santa Barbara, CA 93120

CONTENTS

FOREWORD
Language as a Mask

It was the custom in ancient Greece, India, China and countless other primitive societies to use masks for religious and other rituals. In Japan they were also used extensively for ceremonial occasions. Even today there are Japanese folk traditions where the use of masks of gods, demons and the mythical bird with a long nose are indispensable. By wearing these masks one can transform oneself, so folk tradition tells us, into a greater and more powerful creature. One can become a supernatural being bestowed with a magical power that can perform miracles, such as bringing about a richer harvest, thus serving the community. Dances and short comical plays performed by the masked people were often dedicated to the Shinto shrines.

During the middle ages of Japan, this interdependence between the masks and the ritualistic performance had been developed into a unique form of theater called Noh. Because all the actors were men, from its outset Noh depended for its character portrayal on the use of masks. The earlier masks were of demons, goblins, old men which were also used as gods, and young boys. The masks representing women's faces both young and old came into use last of all; yet it was this particular type of mask that contributed most to the Noh theater when Zeami (c. 1394-1468) was developing it to perfection. Without those beautifully curved female masks, some of which are still used today and ranked as national treasures, Zeami could not have created the renowned Mugen Noh (The Noh of Dream and Illusion). And it is in this Mugen Noh that Yugen, the quality of beauty Noh aspires to communicate—that everlasting atmosphere of twilight charged with deep emotions—is presented in its highest form.

A shite or protagonist, dressed in elaborate silk costume, wearing a wig of long black hair tied at the back and a woman's mask barely big enough to cover the front portion of the actor's face, sits quietly on the stage while the chorus narrates a story. The story often tells the fate of a young beautiful woman whose spirit comes back to hover about a travelling priest, appealing her never-ending sorrow and asking for consolation from him. Shite then dances a calm yet sensual dance in slow symbolic movements. The stage is a reality in one act, then, a dream in the next. The female mask represents a living woman with emotions of sadness, joy, delusion, aspiration; even so, by its very nature, the mask can lend a magical power to the actor who wears it allowing him to step over the threshold of the supernatural.

Hisao Kanze, the late Noh master, wrote in one of his essays that an actor is somewhat like a soul that hovers in the twilight zone between the worlds of reality and death, and it is essential *that he should have something to which he can entrust his whole being. And that something, a mask in this case, must give him magical power.*

To wear a mask in Noh terms, kakeru, *means "to hang" (something) but it also can mean "to cast" (a spell). And a mask,* omote, *means a face as well as a surface. Then by wearing a woman's mask an actor can cast the spell of a woman's spirit over himself.*

Kanze describes his own experience with masks.

> *I cannot even see very well with a mask on. And I know that the slightest movement of my head changes the angle of the mask, thus presenting to the audience an expression of the mask that might be inappropriate at the particular moment. Indeed we actors work with all kinds of restrictions, but in spite of them, or rather because of them, we can cease to be concerned too much with exterior mimicry, and enter, explore and understand our inner world. This makes it possible for the magic to take place on the stage. An actor becomes superhuman and he is able to transform the whole theater into another universe. (p. 104, Hisao Kanze,* Kakoro yori Kokoro ni Tsutauru Hana, Hakusui-sha, *Tokyo, 1979.)*

A mask for a good Noh actor then, is not only one of the theatrical tools needed for technical reasons, but also an indispensable medium through which he can invoke a magical power that enables him to transcend the whole theatrical experience into the realm of the extraordinary, the realm of dream.

In the last ten years, translating Anaïs Nin (into Japanese) and Kanoko Okamoto (into English), I have become aware of the very special ways they use language in their fiction. Language becomes almost like Kanze's female mask in Mugen Noh. It is a tool, and also a medium in which they have found a magical power.

Language, like the Noh masks, can be a supremely liberating artifice. Stylization, while it may seem to cover over or separate from known reality, can bring both writer and reader—or actor and audience—closer to the expansive yet elusive inner emotional world, the world of dream.

When Nin writes: "The vegetation no longer concealed its breathing, its lamentations. The sand no longer concealed its desire to enmesh, to stifle; the sea showed its true face, its insatiable craving to possess;" (p. 171, Winter of Artifice, The Swallow Press, Chicago, 1948), *the vegetation, sand and the sea suddenly become alive with a strange power which silently but recklessly invades our feelings. A passage from Kanoko Okamoto's* The North Country *reads: "There was a barbershop with an old-fashioned signpost of red and white. By the shop was a weeping willow with its voluptuous branches almost touching the earth." In these few lines we realize that the atmosphere of an old small town is set and the theme of sorrow and sensuous passion is subtly introduced.*

In contrast to the free and intimate language Nin uses in her diaries, language that flows like a river with soft murmurs and occasional raging rapids, the language she chooses for her fiction has a distinct character. It is screened through the process of an artistic distillation. Each and every word is chosen with utmost care to create an iridescent veil between the writing and the reader. Seen through this veil, everything takes on a symbolic and magical air.

Nin seldom lingers on realistic descriptions of the ordinary but always penetrates directly into the very core of her theme, human emotions, especially women's, and seeks to convey her basic messages through the use of images, impressions, allusions— qualities so vividly alive in dreams. And the reader is carried into the world of trans-reality, the world of the subconscious, the dream where the fascinating and frightening treasure of emotional experience can be discovered.

On the other hand, Kanoko Okamoto does not hesitate to rely on a detailed description of the places where the dramas take place or the clothes characters wear. But all of these descriptions are necessary in terms of her fictional structure. While she is seemingly dwelling upon straightforward descriptions of a town or mountains, she is preparing the reader, by creating sense images of shape, color, smell or sound, for the inner emotional drama that is to come.

When Henry Miller read my translation of "The Story of an Old Geisha," he said rather disappointed, "But nothing actually happens in the story. . . ." I was a little baffled by this comment, because I had felt that the story had such a strong appeal. I thought that an extremely poignant drama was enacted in the inner self of the old geisha. But of course, Henry Miller is right in a sense, for there is no exterior conflict or struggle taking place among the characters. No one passionately falls in love, no one dies a tragic death.

The old geisha's calm face is presented rather casually. Yet if we can see through it, we realize that behind this mask are hidden her deepest emotional dramas. Behind the facade of an understanding, mature old woman, we see her sadness at becoming old, her enormous sense of loss for not living a full life, her strong will trying tenaciously to hold onto the life-force of youth to bloom once again. She may well be a shite *with a serene female mask in Mugen Noh, who is just an anonymous village woman in the first act, and in the second, reveals her true identity in the dream of a bystander. She is the spirit of a woman, long dead, whose deep-rooted delusions for unfulfilled love give her soul no rest, but force her to linger in the twilight world where the souls of others, perhaps more courageous than hers, can at last fulfill her dreams.*

Anaïs Nin's relationship with Japan is a rather strange one. As a young child she was fascinated by the illustrated Voyage Autour du Monde. *In her twenties she read* The Tale of Genji *(we don't know whose translation it was) and dismissed it as "a thinly disguised imitation of a French novel," (p. 227, Early Diary, III) being unaware that it was written in the 11th century. Later in her sixties she read many Japanese novels in English translation. But unfortunately, she says, "they as a whole failed to bring me any closer to them (Japanese women)" (p. 8, Diary VII), perhaps because so few modern works by Japanese women were translated then. Yet when she finally went to Japan in 1966 at the invitation of the Japanese publisher who introduced her novel,* A Spy in the House of Love, *she immediately fell in love with the country and the women.*

Diary VII *opens with delightful description of her visit to Japan. She also wrote an essay on Japanese women and children in* In Favor of the Sensitive Man. *Henry Miller told me Anaïs said after her visit to Japan that if she had been able to choose, she would have chosen to live in Japan.*

I wish Anaïs could have read Kanoko's stories. She would have loved them. She would have loved the beauty of Kanoko's language. She would have loved the feminine sensitivity, the mute yet passionate love Kanoko's women extend to other human beings. She would have understood these relationships subdued, yet firm, intensive and lasting.

I do not believe that after death we perish into nothingness. I would like to believe that the souls of the dead often come back to visit the living like invisible butterflies or like the large white flowers of cereus that bloom only at night with a sweet and sensual aroma. At times I find myself talking with Anaïs as I used to do, but now in silence. She is perhaps saying that she is very pleased this particular essay is once more available to the world to read, because it so clearly expresses her reasons for giving that special dream quality to her writing. And I believe Anaïs would find in Kanoko a sensitive artist of equal temperament and perhaps a dear friend.

—**Kazuko Sugisaki**

SUSHI

I N THE City of Tokyo, one occasionally comes upon sections where downtown meets residential areas. Leaving the bustling, gay boulevards and entering suddenly into these quiet sections, one has a feeling of coming into a totally different world. In such quarters those who have become tired of the stimuli of new, wide boulevards find a welcome change of mood.

Fukuzushi, a small sushi restaurant, is located at the bottom of a hill in one of these quarters. The building is not new, but the front part of the two-story house was remodeled, and copper was used for the facade. The rest of the house, the living quarters of the family, remains old except for a few new supporting poles on the steep hillside.

The restaurant itself has been there for some time, but the previous owner could not make a go of the business, and sold it, name and all, to Tomoyo's father who seemed to know how to run the place. The business, small as it is, now prospers.

14

The new owner, Tomoyo's father, is an excellent chef who studied and worked in one of Tokyo's top-class restaurants and knows just what quality of sushi will suit the customers. Before Tomoyo's father took over, it had been a take-out sushi shop, but he changed the character of the shop so that customers began to sit at the counter or at the small tables. Soon the work became more than members of the family could handle, so the owner hired a chef, an apprentice and a waitress.

All sorts of people came to the restaurant, but they had one thing in common: they were all hard-pressed people caught up in the reality of everyday living, yet who wanted to get away, if only for a brief moment. Sitting at the bar and ordering sushi, they could have it prepared exactly as they wanted. It was a luxury, not on a grand scale but a luxury all the same. Besides, here one could be a fool. One could wear a mask or expose oneself. If someone said something foolish, no one would disapprove. People regarded each other with the familiarity of those who play hide-and-seek with harsh reality. There was even a kind of protective warmth with which one watched another customer's hands picking up sushi or handling a tea cup.

Sushi creates a strange atmosphere; it is diligent, fast, sound and thoughtful. People can indulge in it as much as they want without spoiling or slowing down its rhythm. The atmosphere is fluid and airy.

The steady customers of Fukuzushi were diverse. There was a man who used to own a gunshop, a sales manager of a department store, a dentist, a son of a *tatami* merchant, a broker who sold telephone bonds, an engineer who designed plaster casts, a toy salesman, a man promoting rabbit meat, an old retired stock broker. And there was still another, who, they supposed, was in some kind of show business, but did side jobs when not appearing in the theater. He came in his oily silk kimono and used his hands deftly to pick up sushi from the counter.

Steady customers often dropped by on their way to and from the barber shop. Businessmen like to come in after business hours. Though it varied with the seasons, the crowd began to gather around four o'clock in the afternoon, and the busy hours continued until dusk when lights began to shine in the houses.

Each chose his favorite seat. Some enjoyed *sake* with hors d'oeuvres such as *sashimi* and marinated fish and vegetables while others would start sushi right away.

One afternoon, Tomoyo's father came out from his place behind the bar with a huge plate of pressed sushi with darkish colored slices of fish on top, and placed the plate in the center of the table.

"What is this?"

"Well, try and see." The owner talked to his customers as if they were his good friends. "I enjoy it with my nightcap."

"It tastes too rich for *kohada*," said one who ventured to eat a piece.

"Could it be Spanish mackerel?"

They heard somebody laugh. It was Tomoyo's mother sitting in the corner of the raised *tatami*-room. She was laughing, shaking her plump body. "You are tricked by Father!" It was very cheap salted mackerel Tomoyo's father used. He had removed the excessive salt and oil by preserving it in bean-curd remains.

"Well, I declare! Aren't you cunning to make such delicious sushi and enjoy it all alone?"

"Really, mackerel tastes quite different when prepared like this!"

The conversation had suddenly become animated.

"You see, since I cannot afford expensive fish..." said the owner.

"Why don't you serve it every day?" one of the customers asked.

"You've got to be kidding! If I did, who would want to order expensive fish? And if that should happen...well, how can I make a profit selling this cheap stuff?"

"So you know your business well!"

Occasionally, unusual dishes such as the white roe of red snapper, intestines of abalone, the bony part of bonito left after the good filet had been taken off, were skillfully prepared and served to the steady customers. When Tomoyo saw these dishes she frowned and said, "How can you eat such things? They taste so awful!"

These Fukuzushi specials came out when least expected. The owner totally disregarded his customers' requests and served them only when he felt like it. Knowing his whims and stubbornness, the customers had learned not to push the owner. When they really craved a dish, they whispered to Tomoyo, and she would find it for them rather grudgingly.

The daughter, Tomoyo, grew up watching these men and had acquired a notion that the affairs of the world were generally not too serious, but easy-going or even playful. In her high school days, she was ashamed to belong to a family that ran a small sushi shop and took great care that none of her classmates saw her go in and out of her home. This was never easy and, at times, could be nerve-racking. It might have been this experience that gave her a rather lonely look, but it also might have come from observing her parents' relationship.

Tomoyo's father and mother never quarrelled, but it seemed to her that their hearts were completely independent of each other. They lived together out of necessity to survive in the world. And yet, the way they cooperated and took care of each other was more instinctive than businesslike. They did it so quietly and masterfully that it seemed that they were reflecting each other's actions. This is why they appeared to others as a quiet and well-matched couple.

Father had an ambition. He wanted to open up a new branch in one of those highrise buildings downtown, but at the same time, he drew considerable pleasure in caring for the little birds he collected. Mother, neither taking pleasure trips nor buying new kimonos, was saving money for herself from their monthly profit. But they shared one common interest, their daughter, Tomoyo. They agreed that Tomoyo should receive a good education. Since society tended to emphasize intellectual values, they felt they had to compete. As the father was only a chef, the daughter had to be something more, but as to how much more, they had no definite idea.

Tomoyo grew up to be a pretty young woman. She seemed to be well acquainted with worldly affairs but had, in fact, only superficial knowledge. She was still an inexperienced young woman, happy but lonely.

No one could really dislike a girl like this. For a time, however, her casual attitude towards men caused concern among her high-school teachers. She was very frank with men and not shy at all. She did not hesitate to talk with them in any way she pleased, which was very unusual for a teenage girl. This puzzled and worried the teachers at first. But after they discovered that it was part of her upbringing as the daughter of a sushi chef who needed her daily help, they accepted her as she was.

One day a school excursion took Tomoyo to the bank of the Tama River. It was early spring. She looked into a little pool of water by the bank where the flow of the river almost stopped. The pool appeared an intense light green like the color of new tea leaves. Several small silver carp came floating into the pool waving their tails and fed on the green moss of a pole. They stayed there for a short while and swam away. Immediately another group of fish, the sun reflecting off their tails, came into the pool again, and then were gone. The fish in the pool never stayed the same, but the change was so swift and quiet that it looked to the human eye as though the same group had always been there. Sometimes, an idle catfish came to join them.

Tomoyo thought that the customers of her shop and the fish she saw in the spring river had something in common. Fukuzushi had steady customers but even they did not stay the same. And she felt she was like the green moss on the pole. The customers would come and go, comforted by being near her.

She did not think of her work at the shop as a duty. Wearing a cashmere uniform that hid the shape of her breasts and hips and dragging old, clip-clap wooden men's sandals, she carried hot green tea to the tables. When someone teased her, venturing to hint his interest in her as a woman, she would pout her lips, shrug one shoulder, and say, "I don't know... how can I answer such a question?"

At such times the nuance of coquetry in her voice was ever so slight but undeniable. Then the customer would laugh, feeling something warm had touched his heart. To that extent, Tomoyo was a maiden of attraction at Fukuzushi.

Among the steady customers there was a Mr. Minato, a middle-aged gentleman. An air of loneliness about his eyebrows cast a shadow over his face. He must have been over fifty. At times he looked much older, and yet on other occasions he looked like a young man with warm, passionate feelings. He had a rather stern face, softened by the hint of resignation with which he regarded the world. One could see he had a keen intellectual sense that illuminated his personality, and that sense added to his resigned attitude. He had thick, curly hair which he parted neatly. He also had a French-style mustache. He usually wore a homespun jacket and a pair of red shoes often covered with dust. Occasionally, he wore a striped silk kimono of good quality.

He was certainly a bachelor. But nobody knew what he did. At Fukuzushi he was simply called *Sensei**. He knew all about sushi. He knew how to enjoy it, but at the same time he did not pretend to be a connoisseur. Entering the shop he tapped the floor with his cane. Then he sat down on one of the stools in front of the bar,

*a general term that is applied to any person of an intellectual or masterful profession

and leaning over the counter he would examine the various fish in the glass case prepared for the day. As he received a teacup from Tomoyo, he said, "I see you have lots of variety today."

"The yellowtail has good fat in it today, and the clams are also good."

When Minato came in, Tomoyo's father would unconsciously begin to wipe off the cutting board and the lacquered surface of the serving board with a clean cotton cloth. The chef had learned that *Sensei* was fastidious.

"Fine, I'll begin with those."

"Yes, sir!"

Tomoyo's father spoke in a more polite way to Minato without really noticing it. He now remembered the course of sushi Minato usually followed. It began with *chutoro**, then cooked fishes garnished with sauce, next light-tasting fishes with blue scales such as mackerel, and finally egg custard and some kind of seaweed roll. To this course the chef would add Minato's special orders for the day in their suitable places.

Between eating and drinking tea, Minato held his hand against his cheek or rested his chin on the back of his hands folded over the head of his cane. He would cast a fixed gaze to the back of the shop towards a pond half hidden by green leaves. The dividing screens were opened up so that you could see the pond from the stools. Or his gaze rested sometimes on the thick oak leaves which covered the wall across the street where Tomoyo took care to water every day.

*the part of tuna with a moderate amount of white fat in it

Tomoyo felt uneasy with Minato at the beginning, but then as she watched him stare absently at those places she began to miss him looking at her. Sometimes Minato did not seem to notice her from the time she brought tea to him until he left. She felt neglected then. On the other hand, if their eyes met and stayed looking at each other for a long time, Tomoyo felt his stare deprived her of strength. She liked it best when their eyes met, as if by chance, only for a moment, and she found him smiling at her. On such occasions Tomoyo felt *emotional vibrations* from him. The vibrations, vague but warm, could dissolve her tension. It was different from the emotions she received from her parents.

When Minato ignored her, Tomoyo stopped her needle point and from her corner by the water heater faked some coughs and made deliberate noises. She did this just to draw Minato's attention, though she was unaware of it. Startled, Minato looked towards her, then his lips stretched smoothly over well-occluded teeth to form a pleasant smile with one tip of his mustache considerably raised. Her father looked up from his busy hands, but recognizing it was only Tomoyo's little trick, continued making sushi with his sullen face unchanged.

Minato talked with other steady customers openly, and they got along well. They talked about horse races, the stock market, politics, the game of *go*, chess and *bonsai*, among other things. Minato seldom opened his mouth, letting others do most of the talking. He did not look down upon them nor was he bored with the conversation, for his manners proved otherwise.

When, for instance, he was offered a cup of *sake*, he received it in his slender, firm hand, gesturing in a way that showed how much he appreciated it. He said, "Actually, my doctor said I shouldn't drink, but since you are so kind to offer, I will gladly accept." Minato emptied the cup, thoroughly enjoying it, then returned it to the customer who had offered it. He lifted a small porcelain bottle and poured *sake* into the customer's cup. Minato's hand movements showed refinement.

Minato's attitude on these occasions made it clear that he really enjoyed people, that he was on good terms with them and could not help returning kindness. So it was agreed among the steady customers that *Sensei* was a very nice person indeed.

But Tomoyo was not particularly happy to see Minato behave this way. He was diminishing his own personality, she felt, to respond so heartily to anyone's whim. He was exhausting his own resources over something rather unimportant. Why did he have to act like an old man craving human warmth rarely shown to him? At such times even Minato's silver ring with an ancient Egyptian scarab seemed detestable to her. Once, a customer, overjoyed by Minato's sincere reception, kept on exchanging cups with Minato who was laughing, obviously enjoying himself. Tomoyo stood up, strode to them and snatched the cup from Minato's hand. "You must stop it now; you yourself said your doctor forbade you to drink." She thrust the cup back to the other customer and without saying more went back to her work.

But it was not her concern for Minato's health that made her act like this; it was a curious jealousy.

"So I see Tomoyo can be a good caring wife!"

People laughed and things were let go at that. Minato smiled awkwardly, bowed slightly to the customer and seated himself in his usual position. He picked up the heavy tea cup once again.

Tomoyo found herself thinking of Minato more and more, and occasionally this made her behave strangely. There were times when she ignored him completely. Once when she saw him come in, she deliberately turned away and went to the farthest corner of the shop. Minato smiled lightly at the cold reception. But when Tomoyo could not be seen at all, he looked lonely and gazed more intensely at the street and the green canyon at the back of the house.

One day Tomoyo went to an insect shop with a basket to buy some singing frogs. Her father enjoyed caring for these little creatures and though he was good at it, they occasionally died. It was the beginning of the summer, and the songs of the frogs, inviting coolness, were welcome.

As she approached the shop she saw Minato coming out of it carrying a glass jar. He did not see Tomoyo. He walked slowly, taking great care with the jar. Tomoyo entered the shop and ordered quickly. While the shopkeeper was putting the frogs in the basket, Tomoyo looked to see where Minato was going.

With the basket on her arm Tomoyo hurried out to overtake him. "*Sensei*! Hey, *Sensei*!"

"Tomoyo! Well, well. . . what a surprise to see you! We never meet outside your restaurant."

Walking side by side, they showed their purchases to each other. Minato had bought several ghost fish whose transparent flesh made their skeletons and small sinuous intestines clearly visible.

"Do you live around here?" Tomoyo asked.

"Yes, I live in an apartment right over there, but it's not my permanent home."

Minato said he wanted to invite Tomoyo for tea. They walked about looking for a good cafe, but there were none that suited them.

"We cannot very well go to the downtown Ginza district with this." Minato looked at the glass jar of ghost fish.

"No, no, we can't," Tomoyo said. "But we don't have to find a cafe, we can sit down for a while in a vacant lot."

Minato looked around him and noticed again the season of green now in full bloom. With a big sigh he exclaimed to the sky, "What a wonderful idea!"

Soon after they turned away from the wide boulevard, they found a vacant lot where a hospital once stood. The building burned down some time ago. The half-collapsed brick wall gave the appearance of a Roman ruin. They put down their purchases and sat down on the grass, throwing their legs out.

Tomoyo had thought she had many things she wanted to ask him. But now, sitting with him like this, they seemed unimportant. She felt very peaceful and calm as if enveloped in a mist. Minato, on the contrary, was quite animated.

"You look very grown up today, Tomoyo!" He was in a good mood. Tomoyo fumbled for a word, and then thought of a question to ask, not an important one, by any means, but to start a conversation.

"Do you really like sushi?"

"I am not sure...to tell you the truth."

"Then why do you come so often to our place to eat it?"

"I didn't mean I dislike sushi. I am rather fond of it. But you see, it comforts me to eat sushi even when I don't particularly want it."

"But why?"

Minato began to tell Tomoyo why it was so.

It may be that a strange child could be born into an old, decaying family. Or perhaps a child feels more keenly a premonition of the fall of the house. Or even that a child, still in the mother's womb, is afflicted by such a strong premonition.

Even when he was very little, he did not like sweet things. He ate only salted rice crackers for snacks. He brought his upper and lower teeth close together and carefully bit into the flat, round shape of a cracker. If the cracker was dry and hard as it should be, it made a nice crunching sound. He chewed slowly and carefully before he swallowed it. Now he was ready for the second bite. Again, he brought his upper and lower teeth close together and cautiously inserted the edge of the cracker between them. But before he bit, he would close his eyes so that he could listen better.

"Crunch!" He knew there were many different tones of the same little "crunch," and when he made the exact tone he liked best, he was so happy that his whole body shook with joy. Then he would stop eating for a while, hold a cracker in his hands, and think. . . his eyes would wet with tears.

The child lived with his parents, a brother and a sister, both older than he, and a maid. The whole family considered him an odd child. His eating habits were unbalanced. He disliked fish.

There were only certain vegetables he could eat. He could not stand the sight of meat.

The father, who hid his nervous tension under a pretense of easy manners, occasionally came to check on what the boy was eating. "How is he doing? Eating well enough to survive?"

The father was simply letting his old prestigious house fall without making any effort to revive it. The changing times made the existence of such a house difficult, but also the father's character created the fall. Despite his inner cowardice, he preferred to put on an air of grandiosity and say, "Oh no, no...no need to worry; our money is inexhaustible." He refused to see the problem; he could not admit defeat.

On the boy's small table were plain scrambled eggs and some dried seaweed. The mother hid the plate from her husband's prying eyes and said, "Please, don't make a fuss. If you do, he will not even be able to eat these things. He is so bashful."

It was actually painful for the child to eat. He felt the lumps of food with their color, smell and taste would contaminate his body. He wished for food as pure as air. Having nothing in his stomach he often felt hungry. He was starving, yet, afraid to eat. Then he would put his cheek on a cold marble art object in the alcove, stick out his tongue and lick it. He knew he would faint from hunger. But when his fainting spell came, the boy did not mind it at all. It happened just as the sun set behind the hill beyond the little pond in the valley (the geography of the child's neighborhood was much like that of Fukuzushi's). He felt he could die at that instant and not regret it. He put his hands under the obi sash tied tightly

around his empty belly, turned his face upward, bent forward, and
cried out, "Mother!"

But he was not calling his own mother. He liked his present
mother best of all in the family, and yet he had the feeling that
there was a woman somewhere else, a woman whom he could call
his "Mother." But at the same time, if that woman should hear his
cry and come out to see him, he would not be able to face the
shock of seeing her in person. But still he felt some sad comfort in
calling to the woman, "Mother! Mother. . . ." His voice was like
thin paper trembling in a wind.

"Yes, dear, are you calling me?" The child heard a voice
answering his call. It was the mother he knew. "Oh, poor child,
what's the matter with you? All alone in such a place!" She
grabbed his shoulders and shook them. She looked into the boys'
face. He was embarrassed by the mistake this mother made and
blushed a little.

"This is why I want you to eat three good meals a day. Now,
you understand, don't you? I really wish you would eat properly!"

He realized this mother was terribly upset because her voice
was shaking.

The mother discovered after much anxiety and worry that the
only foods the child could eat were eggs and dried seaweed. He
could swallow them because, even though they made his stomach
heavy, he felt they did not taint his body. At times he was
suffocated by an inexplicable, dark oppression filling his entire
body. He wanted to bite into anything sour and soft and so, picked
green plums and small unripe tangerines. When the rainy season

of May came, he knew as well as a bird where to find these fruit trees.

The boy did well at school. He had a photographic memory, but was bored with the lessons. Everything was too easy. His boredom and cold, standoffish attitude towards the whole learning process somehow made him all the more distinctive at school. His teachers and classmates treated him differently. At home too, he was considered odd.

One day his parents quarrelled bitterly behind closed doors. His mother came out and took the child aside. She was very serious, and her face was stern.

"Now listen to me, my dear, your teachers are concerned about you because you are so thin and still losing weight. They think your parents are not taking good care of you, not paying enough attention to your health. Your father has heard of this, and. . .you know how he is, he has blamed me for everything."

Then, the mother sat down in front of the boy, and putting her palms flat on the *tatami* floor, bowed to him. "Please, I beg you, dear, please try to eat more so that you'll gain weight and become healthier. Otherwise, I don't think I can stay here. I feel I have no place in this house."

The boy felt he had committed the ultimate evil, one his ill-formed character had prefigured. His conscience pained him, for he had caused his own mother to bow to him, and in such a humiliating way, with her hands down on the floor. His face flushed and his body began to shake, though inside, he was quite calm.

"I have committed an unforgivable wrong against my mother,"
he thought, "I am evil and might as well be dead. I shall not mind
if I die now. So I'll eat anything. If unfamiliar things make me
vomit, make my body impure and rot, I will not regret it. I would
be better off dead than alive. I am a big trouble to other people as
well as to myself." Thus resolved, he sat down at the dinner table
with the rest of the family and ate what they ate.

Immediately he started to vomit. He tried to make his tongue
and throat numb so as not to taste anything. As soon as he
swallowed a mouthful, the thought that the food he had just
swallowed was prepared by women other than his mother
wrenched his stomach. The image of the maid's red underwear
flashing through her *kimono* and an image of the darkish hair oil
dripping down the cheek of the old woman who cooked rice,
tumbled violently through his mind.

His brother and sister looked at him with disgust. The father
merely glanced at him out of the corner of his eye and kept on
emptying his *sake* cup. The mother hurriedly cleaned up the mess.
She looked up at her husband's face reproachfully and sighed,
"You see, it's not my fault, he is like this, he cannot eat ordinary
things." But still she acted timidly toward her husband.

The next day the mother brought out a new *tatami* mat and
spread it in the corridor where the young, thick leaves of the
garden cast a shadow. She also had a cutting board, a knife, a
wooden bowl and a miniature screened cupboard. They were all
new, she had just bought them herself. The mother made the boy
sit down in front of his little dining table on the other side of the
cutting board. On the table she put a plate. She tucked her sleeves

up high, stretched her arms forward and showed him her clean rosy palms. She turned her hands over a few times like the gesture of a stage magician. Rubbing her palms together rhythmically, she said, "Now watch this. Everything I have here is new and clean. The cook is your mother. My hands have been scrubbed and washed thoroughly. Do you see? Okay? Now then, let me see...." The mother started to mix sweet vinegar with warm rice. Both mother and child coughed from the sour steam evaporating from the bowl. The mother drew the bowl of rice to her side, took a small handful of rice and made it into an oval shape. In the screen cupboard, various sushi ingredients were neatly prepared on a plate. She took one piece out, quickly placed it on the rice ball, pressed it lightly and put it down on the child's plate. It was sliced egg custard sushi. "There, it's sushi, you can eat it with your hand."

The child ate it with his fingers. The mouthful of vinegar-seasoned warm rice gave him the sensation that his naked skin was caressed gently and softly by warm hands. The sweet taste of egg custard mingled with warm rice spread over his tongue. He chewed it, swallowed it and savored it. Suddenly he was delighted by this delicious food his mother was giving him for it brought him close to her. He was so happy that he felt he could rub his body against her's. The delicious taste of sushi and his love for his mother mingled together in him like warm scented water, and filled his whole body.

The boy was too shy to say he liked it. He smiled awkwardly and looked up at his mother's face. She knew he liked it. "Well then, I'll make another for you." Again she stretched out her arms, showed her rosy palms, flipped them over in the same magician's gesture. She took out one slice and pressed it on the small rice ball. The boy looked at the white slice on the rice but was repulsed. Seeing him hesitate, the mother said with an air of authority that was not too frightening, "This is nothing to be afraid of. Think of it as white egg custard."

It was the very first time that the boy had eaten a slice of squid. It was smooth as ivory, and he could chew it more easily than just pounded white rice cake. In the middle of this great adventure of chewing a squid sushi, he let out a deep breath which for so long he had held within him. And he felt his face relax for the first time. He liked the flavor very much, but he did not say so. He only smiled.

The mother set out a piece of transparent fish for the next sushi. The boy picked it up with his fingers and brought it to his mouth. As he did so, the smell of it frightened him a little, but he held his breath to block the smell, and summoning all his courage, put it in his mouth. To his surprise, the tiny white transparent piece was a delicious, unknown taste. As he chewed, he felt nutrition suddenly bestowed upon him. He swallowed it down his thin throat.

"It must have been a real fish," he thought. Then he felt the new strength of a conqueror who has killed an animal by tearing it apart alive. He wanted to look around and reassure himself of his new strength. Moved by this unknown delight he raised his hands to the sides of his belly and scratched with dancing fingers.

"Hee, hee, hee..." the child laughed a strange high-pitched laugh.

The mother knew that victory was now hers. She picked grains of rice off her hands slowly, one by one, and with a deliberate calmness looked into the cupboard.

"What shall I make next? Let me see. . . is there any more left? I wonder. . . ."

The child could hardly wait for the next sushi. He was screaming now, "Sushi! Sushi!"

The mother hid her joy and kept a vacant look on her face, which the boy liked most of all. She looked so beautiful at such times that he had never forgotten it.

"Well, since my guest requests it, I shall make more sushi for him."

She again extended her rosy hands before his eyes and, flipping them over like a magician, made another sushi. It was made with a slice of white fish, like the one before. She had chosen fish with very little color and smell for the initial venture: bream and flounder. The boy kept eating one after another. They were racing now. As soon as the mother had made one sushi and put it down on his plate, the boy's fingers picked it up. The race made them oblivious to everything around them, drawing them into a passionate numbness. A delightful rhythm manipulated the movements of their hands.

The mother, not being a professional chef, could not possibly make all the pieces in even shapes. Sometimes a piece rolled sideways and dropped the fish slice on the plate. The boy loved it all the more when this happened. He picked up the fish, put it on top of the rice ball and rearranged the shape himself before eating it. It tasted even better when he did that.

The image of the phantom mother he had been secretly calling and this mother who was now making sushi for him, became superimposed, almost one. Was it happening in his imagination, or was it an optical illusion? He was not sure. He wanted the two images to become one, of course; but on the other hand, if that actually happened, he would have been scared. . . . Could it be that the phantom mother he had been secretly calling was the same as this mother who was now giving him such delicious food? If so, he was sorry, very sorry that he had betrayed her and transferred his love and affection to another woman.

"That should be enough for today. Thank you, dear, I am glad you ate so well!" The mother clapped her hands with happy satisfaction.

After this success the mother did the same thing several times, and the boy grew accustomed to the mother's home-made sushi. He could eat sushi with a red-clam which looked like a pomegranate flower, or he could eat a half-beak, a small slender fish with two silver lines on its back. Gradually he had learned to eat other things served at the regular family dinners. His health improved astonishingly. By the time he was in high school, he was a magnificently beautiful young man.

His father's attitude suddenly changed. Before he had been standoffish and cold to the son, but now he took a sudden interest in him. He made the son sit at the dinner table with him, and made him drink *sake*. He took him to a billiard hall and to a traditional restaurant and called geisha to serve them. All this time, the family was rapidly losing its financial foundation. The prestigious house was collapsing. But the father, ignoring this grim fact, chose to enjoy watching his beautiful son, wearing a blue cotton kimono with white dots, drink *sake* slowly from a small porcelain cup. He was proud that his son was the center of attention of all the women he knew. Thus at sixteen he was already an accomplished playboy.

The mother, who had given the son so much love and care, who had gone through so much trouble just to keep him alive, furiously accused her husband.

"You've corrupted him! You've thoroughly corrupted him!"

The father answered her desperate fury with his wry smile. The son had only contempt and disgust for the parents who quarelled bitterly as if to forget the oppressive fact of the house's decline.

The son did very well at school. Every lesson was almost too easy for him. Without making any effort, he stayed at the top of his class. He had no difficulty entering one of the best universities in Tokyo. Even so he could not shake off a kind of sad emptiness, a void he did not know how to fill. He looked for something, but a hasty search proved unfulfilling. After a long period of boredom, he graduated from the university and found himself a job.

His family was completely ruined and passed out of existence. Both parents died, and his brother and sister followed them soon after. The son, who was capable enough, had no difficulty in finding or keeping a job. He made good advances in his work, but somehow he could not find satisfaction in climbing the ladder to the top company positions. He could not take any profession or business seriously. Nothing really interested him.

When he was about fifty, his second wife died. Around that

time he had a lucky break in the stock market and acquired enough money to live comfortably for the rest of his life. So he quit his job, stopped working altogether, and gave up his home. Ever since, he has been moving from one apartment to another, not wanting to stay in one place too long.

"I am the child, the boy, and eventually, the young man in this story," said Minato after his long narration.

"I see..." Tomoyo answered, "that's why you like sushi so much."

"Well, actually, when I was grown up, I didn't enjoy it as much as I did before. But recently, memories of my mother come back to me so often. It may be that I myself am getting old, you know...and whenever I think of my mother, I remember sushi, too."

A wisteria arbor grew at the corner of the burnt hospital's remains. One of the supporting poles had collapsed and the twisted vines of the tree hung down to the ground. Even so, young leaves sprouted from the tips of the vines, and the cluster of flowers bloomed like drops of purple dew. An azalea bush remained. It used to decorate the base of a rock in the former garden. The rock was carried away, but the plant, coming out of the hole with one side burnt, still had white flowers on the healthy branches.

The edge of the garden dropped down steeply, and the railroad ran at the bottom. The noise of the train shook the air from time to time. Purple wall irises among Japanese snake beards were swinging in the evening breeze. The shadow of a fat palm trunk by which they were sitting became long and dark on the grass. The singing frogs in Tomoyo's basket made a song or two that made them smile at each other.

"The afternoon is almost gone. You would like to get home now," Minato said to Tomoyo. Tomoyo stood up with the basket on her arm. Minato lifted the glass jar of ghost fish, gave it to Tomoyo, and turned to go.

After that day, Minato did not come back to Fukuzushi.

"What has happened to *Sensei* these days? We haven't seen him for a long while," some steady customers asked. But soon they forgot him.

Tomoyo regretted that she had not asked where he lived. She did not know how to find him. At times she went to the ruined lot where they sat that afternoon and stood there a while, or sat on a rock remembering Minato. Tears would appear in her eyes. After a while she would walk home slowly, absent-mindedly.... But as time went by, Tomoyo went to the lot less frequently, and finally, not at all.

Now whenever she thinks of Minato, she simply tells herself, "*Sensei* must have moved again and must be going to another sushi restaurant. A sushi place can be found in any neighborhood." Her memory of Minato is already hazy, dim, fading....

(1939)

THE OLD GEISHA
(Rogi Sho)

HER NAME is Sonoko Hiraide, but it does not fit her personality just as the real name of a *Kabuki* actor does not fit. On the other hand, if we call her by her professional name, Kosono, it does not do justice to the dignified grace she has begun to acquire recently in accordance with her wish to give up her profession. Therefore it is better to call her simply old geisha.

Often people see her in department stores in the middle of the day. With a simple western style hairdo and wearing a *kimono* of thick twilled silk in the fashion of an ordinary respectable woman, she walks around the store with a melancholy expression on her face followed only by a small maid. She walks around and around the same area kicking her legs out at each step, dangling her two arms lazily down along her well-built body. Or she speeds as fast and straight as the thread of a kite and stops at an unexpectedly remote counter. She is not aware of anything except the loneliness of the middle of the day.

Though she is not aware of it, she seems to be resting in the solitude of noon. If her bluish oval eyes happen to catch something of interest, they slowly open and focus on the item as though it were a peony in a dream. Her lips twist at the corners as they did in her youth and break momentarily into a smile. Then the melancholy expression returns.

Upon meeting a rival in the geisha quarter her blank look provides only a short pause until she begins to talk fluently and cheerfully.

While the former matron of the Shinkiraku Restaurant was still alive, she, Hisago of Shinbashi, and the old geisha had very witty and animated conversations typical of geisha society. When they were together, even mature geishas would leave the customers and gather around the older women eager to learn such skilled conversation. When she did not have her rivals with her, still the old geisha often talked to the favored young ones about her career.

She told of an embarrassing occasion when she was an apprentice. Once she laughed so much at the frank talk between the guests and her elders that she wet the floor and started crying because she could not stand up. Then, when she became a mistress she eloped with a young man and her old patron took her mother as a hostage. After she established herself as the owner of a modest geisha house, her financial situation was very tight. She had to rent a carriage by the month to get to Yokohama to receive a loan of five yen, but the carriage cost her twelve yen! She would have the young women laughing to the point of exhaustion as she told one incident after another. Though the plots were more or less the same, her storytelling made them hilariously funny. She seemed to be pursuing her listeners, thrusting her nails of enchantment into their flesh as though she were possessed by a demon. Perhaps old age, envious of youth, was torturing youth in a dexterous manner.

The young geishas, their hair now disheveled, held their sides and gasped, "Oh, please, madam, stop it! We will die if you keep us laughing like this!"

The old geisha never talked about living people but made penetrating observations about those now dead with whom she had had intimate relationships. Among these, unexpectedly, were artisans and men of fame.

She related well-known anecdotes even if people wondered whether they were true or not. For instance, when the prominent Chinese actor, Mei Lang-fang, came to Tokyo and played in the Imperial Theater, the old geisha went to the wealthy promoter who had brought the actor from China. She begged the promoter, regardless of the cost, to arrange an occasion for her to see the actor privately. But the promoter managed to persuade her to give up the idea and go home.

One of the young geishas, panting for breath between laughs, said, "Is it true that you took out your bankbook from your *obiage* sash and showed it to him to prove that you had enough money?"

"What nonsense! Did you say *obiage*? I wasn't a child, you know, I didn't need an *obiage* to tie my *obi*."* Then, just like a child, she suddenly became angry. This child-like anger coming

---

*A wide sash to tie the *kimono*.

from the mature geisha was very amusing, so the young geishas often brought up this subject to embarrass her.

"But, you see," the old geisha would say after her long talk, "we are all looking for only one man, no matter how many we have had in our life. When I remember the men I had, I can see that what attracted me to them are parts of this ideal man whom I have always kept in my heart. That's the reason I couldn't have a lasting relationship with any one of them."

"And who is the ideal man you are still looking for?"

"If I knew that, my troubles would be over forever." With her habitual melancholic beauty, she said that it could have been her first lover or it might be someone she would meet someday.

"In a way, I envy ordinary housewives. All they have to do is to be faithful to the man their parents choose for them. They usually have only one man in their lifetime, and think nothing of having children by him, and in their old age, they can depend on the children."

When the old geisha's talk came to this point, the young ones would whisper that though they really enjoyed listening to her, in the end it often tended to be depressing.

During the last ten years, after she became comfortably well off and comparatively free to choose which parties she entertained, Kosono gradually came to prefer a healthy and ordinary life to her professional one. She divided her geisha house completely from her living quarters and built an extra entrance to her quarters that looked like the entrance to an ordinary residential house. She also adopted a girl from a distant relative and sent the girl to high school. Further, Kosono began studies that were more modern and intellectual than those of traditional geisha training.

The old geisha came to me for lessons in *waka**. She had an introduction from a mutual acquaintance who lived in downtown Tokyo. After a brief self-introduction, the old geisha said something like this: A geisha was like a multi-purpose knife. It did not have to be particularly sharp to cut any one way but it definitely had to be able to serve many purposes. She wanted to learn *waka* just enough to get by at refined intellectual's parties. Now that she was no longer young, she had more opportunities to work for such people.

I gave Kosono, who was as old as my mother, *waka* lessons for about a year. Then I discovered that even though she had some feeling for *waka*, her talent was more for *haiku*, so, I introduced her to a *haiku* poet. The old geisha sent her gardener to my house and had him build in the downtown Tokyo fashion a little pond and water fountain in the inner garden as a token of her gratitude.

Kosono had her main living quarters remodeled in half-western style and installed various electric devices. The motivation must have been her sense of rivalry. She had seen them in a newly built restaurant where she entertained a client. When the devices started to work, she felt that there was a healthy and almost mysterious quality in what they could do. When she used an instant water heater that streamed out hot water from the faucet as soon as she poured cold water in it, and an electric ashtray with a lighter which could instantly light tobacco when pushed down

*A traditional short poem with thirty-one syllables.

with the tip of a pipe, the old geisha felt a fresh, unknown thrill.

"They seem to be alive...un huh...well, everything should work in this way."

This feeling she received from electric devices made her imagine a world of exactness and speed, which, in turn, made her reflect on the way she had been living. "What I have been doing was slow and very inefficient like turning the lamp on and off over and over again," she thought. For a while, she got up early every morning looking forward to toying with the devices, though she was annoyed with the rising figures on the electricity bill.

The devices broke down frequently, and Makita, the owner of a neighborhood electric shop, came to repair them. As he worked, the geisha followed him around and watched him with curiosity, and gradually she began to acquire a little knowledge of electricity.

"When plus and minus currents meet together, they can do a lot of things, un huh...it is just like compatibility in the temperaments of people," she said. And after this her admiration for civilization increased all the more.

Makita often came to help her since she did not have a man in her household. One day Makita was accompanied by a young man. Makita introduced him and explained that he would take care of the electric system for her from now on. His name was Yuki. He was a cheerful and carefree young man, and looking around the house he remarked, "There is no *shamisen** in this house, but it is a geisha house, isn't it?"

As his visits became more frequent he became a good-natured

*A traditional instrument with three strings played like a banjo.

rival as a coversationalist, for his carefree attitude and young, refreshing mood suited Kosono's.

"Your work, Yuki, is cheap; it never lasts more than a week." She would use rough expressions talking to him.

"If so, I cannot help it. Petty jobs of this kind don't arouse my passion."

"What is passion?"

"Well, passion is . . . let me see, it means in the terms of your society 'attraction' maybe. I don't feel any attraction to this job."

The old geisha thought of her career for a moment and pitied herself for what she had done in her lifetime. She recalled many parties she worked for and many men with whom she had relationships, feeling no passion whatsoever.

"I see, then what kind of work can attract you?"

The young man said that it would be to invent some new device and get a patent and make a lot of money with it.

"OK, then why don't you do it?"

Yuki looked up at her face.

"'Why don't you do it?' It's not so simple. This is why people call your kind of women playthings. You cannot talk sense."

"No, you are mistaken. I said it because I have already decided to help you. If I can take care of your living expenses, are you willing to devote yourself to what you want to do?"

So, Yuki left Makita's shop and came to live in one of Kosono's rental houses. The old geisha had one of the rooms remodeled into a workshop as Yuki wanted and bought some apparatus for his research and experiments.

Yuki had worked his way through school and finally learned the trade of electrical engineering. But he had his own ambitions and did not wish to be tied down as a mere wage earner. He worked as a temporary helper, which was almost as unrewarding as a day laborer, at various shops in Tokyo until he met Makita, who came from the same town as Yuki and offered him a live-in job. Yuki moved into his household, but Makita's many children and the many small jobs, one after another, drove Yuki to his wit's end. So he immediately accepted the geisha's offer.

However, Yuki was not particularly grateful to her. He thought that any old geisha who had led a pleasure-filled life squeezing easy money out of men would do things like this in her old age to ease her guilty conscience. Although he was not so impudent as to assume that he was doing her a favor by accepting the offer, he did not feel that he owed her anything.

For the first time in his life, he did not have to worry about his daily bread. He was happy in the quiet, constructive life born from his sincere effort to create something new in this world. He spent his days laboriously contrasting texts with the results of experiments and selecting what might be useful for his inventions. He looked at his own image in the mirror. It was an image of a young man with a strong, masculine body (he admitted it himself), wearing a linen shirt and with his hair slightly curled, sitting slanted in a chair and smoking leisurely. He thought that it was a completely diffrent self and that this image was most suitable for a young inventor. An open veranda surrounded the workshop, and in a small rectangular garden beyond there were a few trees.

When he felt exhausted he went out to the veranda, lay down flat on his back, looked up at the sky above the city with its blue a little blurred, and transplanted his many fantasies into dreams.

Kosono came to visit him every few days. She looked around the house, observed what was lacking and then later sent it with a servant.

"You are such a neat person for your age. Your house is always in good order and you never have dirty clothes piled up."

"Naturally, you see, my mother died very young, so even when I was just a baby, I had to change and wash my own diapers."

The old geisha laughed saying that he could not be serious, but then said with a sad face, "But I have heard that if a man is too concerned with trivialities, he cannot make a great success."

"Well, I don't think it is my real nature either. But somehow it has become my habit, and I feel ill at ease when I see untidiness in myself. It bothers me, you know. . . ."

"I don't understand why, but be sure to let me know if you need anything."

On the day of *Hatsuuma** the geisha ordered *inari-zushi*** from a nearby restaurant, and they ate it together enjoying it as if they had been mother and son.

The foster daughter, Michiko, was a capricious girl. She came to see Yuki almost every day and wanted him to keep her company. Growing up in this particular society where love is treated like a commodity, Michiko could not help absorbing this

*The first day of the horse in February.
**Rice balls wrapped in slices of fried bean curd.

commercialism of love, despite her foster mother's effort trying to insulate her from it. She was precocious about love, but only in superficial manners.

She had passed quickly through adolescence without having really been conscious of it. Her heart had hardened while it was still that of a child and was now covered with a thin layer of the discretion of adulthood. Since Yuki was not interested in spending idle time with her, her interest in him diminished and her visits would cease for a long while; then one day she would reappear sluggishly. Here is a young man whom her mother is taking care of, so she had better take advantage of the situation, Michiko thought. On the other hand, she did not seem to approve her mother taking in a total stranger.

Michiko sat on Yuki's lap casually and gave him sidelong glances which were perfect in form but lacking any inner meaning.

"Can you tell how much I weigh?"

Yuki pushed her up and down on his knees a few times. "For your age, marriageable age that is, you lack delicacy of manners."

"No, I don't think so. I got an A in ethics at school."

She might have misunderstood the meaning of what Yuki said or she might have chosen to ignore it.

Yuki lightly felt her body through her clothes. He couldn't help letting out a short laugh because there was something droll about her, as if an undernourished child was trying to imitate the coquettishness of a full-grown woman.

"Oh, you offend me! Of course, you are much too great a person for me!" She stood up angrily.

"Do some exercises and build your body up so that you'll have a body like your mother's."

After this incident Michiko, though she did not know quite why, hated him intensely.

Yuki's sense of happiness continued about half a year. Then he became somewhat absent-minded. While he was only planning his new inventions, the ideas seemed wonderful. However, when he started actual research and experiments, he realized that the kind of things he had in mind had been invented and were already patented. Even if his own invention happened to be more advanced, he would have to change it so that it would not conflict with previously patented ones. Besides he doubted that there was any demand for the things he was inventing. He found out that there were many good inventions, admirable from the professional point of view, which were not used at all; on the other hand, simple devices born from casual ideas were great successes. Although he had some idea that invention would necessarily involve speculation, he had not in the least realized that the ideas and their practical materialization might conflict in such a way.

But, more than anything else, what made him lose interest in this life he was living now was something he felt within himself. While he was working for wages, he could take those trivial jobs day after day, because his ambition was to some day save up enough money to devote himself to his dream, the invention of new things. Thus, when he thought of the bright days to come, he felt in his heart a thrilling anticipation. But once his ambition became reality, he found his daily life boring, almost tormenting.

With a deadly silence around him, he feared that he was left behind, alone, apart from society. In such isolated research he had no one to consult and he might be working in an entirely wrong direction.

Besides, he began to doubt his own wish of becoming rich. He did not have to worry about earning a living any longer. If he went out for a little pleasure, all he wanted to do was to see a movie, enjoy a drink or two at a bar and then take a taxi home in a mellow and gay mood. And the old geisha would willingly give him enough money for this sort of modest spending. For his comfort this was more than enough. A few times, Yuki had gone to a pleasure quarter with his friends, but his enjoyment was superficial. Each time he went, he wished to come home where he could do as he pleased and sleep in his own comfortable bed.

He had never stayed out all night. He bought a bed almost too luxurious for a man in his present situation, and he ordered the best feathers to make the quilt. Sometimes Yuki felt frightened when he realized that he did not have any more desire, no matter how hard he searched within himself, and that his attitudes had become passive. He wondered if he had lost his normal self, normal for his age.

At such times, Yuki's thoughts wandered to the old geisha: What kind of woman is she? Her face always looks melancholy, but she has something indomitable and unyielding in her. Take her lessons, for instance, she is always moving towards new things as if she is trying to devour new ideas one after another. Alternate satisfaction and dissatisfaction are constantly pushing her forward.

The next time Kosono came to see him, Yuki asked her. "Do you know Mistanguette, a very famous night-club entertainer in France?"

"Yes, I've heard her songs on a record.... The way she sings those intricate melodies are just marvelous."

"Well, I was told the old woman has all her wrinkles tucked in the soles of her feet. But I imagine you don't have to do that yet, do you?"

Her eyes glared for an instant, then with a quick smile she said, "Me? Well, the number of my New Years Eve peas* has become so large that I doubt if my skin will act as it used to, but let me see...."

The old geisha, rolling up her sleeve, thrust out her left arm to Yuki. "Pinch the skin on the top of my upper arm with your thumb and forefinger, pinch it tight and hold it."

Yuki did as he was told. Kosono pulled the skin from the bottom with two fingers, then the skin held by Yuki's hand slipped away gently and returned to its original smoothness. Yuki tried it once more, harder this time, but just as before his fingers could not hold the skin. Yuki felt the sturdy mysterious white smoothness was like the belly skin of an eel or white parchment.

"How weird! This is really something!"

The old geisha rubbed off the red mark left by Yuki's fingers with the sleeve of her silk underwear and said, "I owe this to childhood dance training. Teachers used to strike and beat one, you know...."

---

*It is an old custom to eat as many peas as one's age on New Years Eve.

She remembered those hard times and her countenance darkened. Then, staring at Yuki awhile, she said, "What has become of you lately? Don't misunderstand me, I am not saying that I want you to work harder or to become a quick success. But let's say that if you were a fish, you've lost freshness. It's a bit strange to me that you, a young man who should have enough worries of his own, is wondering about the age of an older woman. There is something sardonic about your mind."

Yuki, surprised by her understanding, confessed to her frankly. "If you want to know the truth, I might as well tell you. I am no good anymore. I have lost passion for this world. No, I didn't lose it, I didn't have it from the beginning."

"No, that's not true, you had it, but if this is the way you feel now, it's a problem, isn't it? But you've put on weight, and you are looking much better than you used to."

It is true that Yuki had put some weight on his well-built body, which gave him an air of wealth and rank. In the soft swell of the eyelids above his brown pupils and the corpulent flesh under his chin, a sensuous red began to appear.

"Yes, my physical condition is excellent. I feel so good that, sitting as I am now, I can drop off to sleep, and unless I try very hard to be aware of things, they just slip away from my mind even if they are important. Yet I feel insecure and uneasy all the time. I've never known anything like this before."

"Perhaps you are eating too much *mugitoro**, and the wild white yam is giving you too much energy," the old geisha teased

---

*A dish of ground wild white yam and steamed wheat.

him since she knew that Yuki often had his orders of *mugitoro* delivered from a neighborhood restaurant famous for this special-ty. Then, regaining seriousness immediately, she said, "If this is the case, perhaps you should look for a seed of trouble, any kind of trouble, because sometimes you are better off when you have something to worry about."

A few days after that, the old geisha invited him for an outing. Michiko and two young geishas from another house, whom Yuki did not know, accompanied them. The two geishas were wearing their semi-formal *kimonos*, and they thanked Kosono very politely. "Thank you so very much for today's outing, Madam."

The old geisha said to Yuki, "This is going to be a consolation party for you, and I paid these women's fees for a whole day's outing. So you can enjoy their company as much as you wish."

As expected, the young geishas worked very hard to please Yuki. When they were about to get in the boat at the ferry port at Takeya, the younger geisha asked Yuki, "Could you hold my hand, please?" And when she got in, she staggered on purpose and held on to Yuki's back as if to embrace him. Yuki smelled scented hair oil, and he saw, at his chest height, the plump white nape where the borders of the nape hair were receding into a misty white skin exposed beyond the red lining of her collar. On her thickly made up profile with a cheek that shone like white enamel, a high nose cut a fine line with statue-like clarity.

The old geisha remarked, "What a lovely scene!" Sitting on a shifting board, she took out a tobacco case and a lighter from the folds of her *obi*.

They walked and rode in a taxi, admiring the early summer

scenery along the Arakawa Canal. Factories and residential houses for the factory workers were being built, but the old mood of Kanegafuchi and Ayase still remained here and there like torn pieces on a land of cinders. A few silk trees for which the Ayase River was well known were still standing and boat carpenters were working on a reed island beyond the stream.

"When I was kept in a villa at Mukōjima, my patron was such a jealous man that he did not let me leave this neighborhood. So, I used to tell him that I was just going for a short walk. My lover disguised himself as a carp fisherman and moored his boat under the row of those silk trees by the bank, and on the boat we used to have what you call now a 'rendezvous.'"

She remembered that when the evening came, the flowers of the silk trees began to fold, the sound of the boat carpenters' hammers trailed off, and the pale blue mist hazily floated on the water.

"Once we talked about committing double suicide, and it almost happened, because all we had to do was just to step overboard."

"What made you change your mind?" asked Yuki thumping his feet in the boat.

"Well, you see, we were trying to decide when we would do it. We kept putting it off each time we met. One day a couple of bodies that looked like double suicide corpses reached the opposite shore. They were surrounded by a lot of bystanders. My lover went to take a look at them. When he came back he said, 'Double suicide corpses are not much to look at. I think we'd better drop the idea.' Well, if I had died with my lover, it would have been all right for us, but then, I felt sorry for my patron who would have been left behind. Oh, I disliked him with a passion, but still you feel something for a man when he is so jealous of you."

The young geishas remarked, "We envy you, hearing your stories of those good old days. Things are so dry and frigid nowadays, it's really disgusting."

"No, I don't think so," said the old geisha waving her hand. "You have your own good things today. For instance, things move faster now than they used to, like electricity, you know. Besides there are more techniques you can use. To me things happening today are fascinating."

With subtle encouragement from Kosono, the two geishas again began waiting on Yuki eagerly, making full use of their seductive charms, with the younger one as the main entertainer and the elder, subordinate.

Michiko looked disturbed. In the beginning she was serene, separating herself from the group and showing contempt for them, occasionally taking pictures of the scenery. Then suddenly she began acting very intimately toward Yuki, trying candidly to win his attention from the geishas. Yuki's sensuality was curiously aroused by the thin scent of her flesh, a scent that her desperate aggressiveness barely squeezed out of her immature virgin body. Spontaneously he inhaled a deep breath of air into his lungs. But this excitement was only momentary and it soon left him.

The young geishas did not particularly welcome the challenge from Michiko, but since she was Madam's foster daughter and they were there only professionally, they avoided a vain competition with the daughter. Only when her whim shifted elsewhere did they resume their services. This irritated Michiko as if flies swarmed over her piece of cake. To try to disperse the irritation, Michiko vented it on her mother.

But the old geisha was self-composed, and without paying much attention to what was going on, she calmly picked up chickweeds on the bank for her canaries and drank beer with cooked taro at a teahouse of the Iris Garden. Evening came and they were to have dinner at a restaurant in the precinct of the Water God Shrine, but Michiko stopped at the gate and stared boldly at Yuki. "I am going home, I don't feel like eating a Japanese dinner."

The young geishas were surprised and said that they should take her home in that case. Kosono laughed, "Don't make such a fuss. We can just put her in a taxi," and she stopped a taxi that came along. Watching the car drive away, the old geisha said, "She has learned a few smart tricks, hasn't she?"

What the old geisha was doing for him confused Yuki more and more. He knew now that his first interpretation of her intention was mistaken. She was not being good to a young man because she wished to ease her sense of guilt. She had never given any hint that she wanted him as her gigolo, which was now the inevitable neighbors' gossip. Why was her attitude so permissive toward him?

Yuki seldom went to the workshop now where his research had been long neglected. The old geisha, understanding it all very well, did not say a word to Yuki, which puzzled him all the more about her purpose in helping him. Then, she was not patronizing a young inventor, either. He lay down on the veranda and avoided looking into his workshop through the glass screen which divided the two areas.

Now that early summer was here, fresh green leaves were sprouting from the old trees in the garden. The azalea and wall iris by the stone at the edge of the buried pond were calling for wasps. The sky was clear and profoundly blue. A raindrop-pregnant cloud of a dull color in the shape of a continent was slowly moving. *Paulownia* flowers bloomed in the garden of a neighbor.

Yuki remembered with sweet melancholy his working days when he went to many strange houses. Once he repaired a connection in a narrow kitchen closet where he could hardly move his arms and the smell of a moldy soy sauce barrel filled the place. Or he had lunch in strangers' houses with a dish or two given to him by a wife or a maid. He remembered he really detested those things then. Once when he was working on an estimate of a new order in Makita's upstairs room, the children came up in turns and hugged him so hard that his neck was swollen red. One of the children took a piece of candy from her mouth and, with her saliva dripping from it like a thread, pushed it into his mouth.

Yuki began to wonder if what he wanted actually was to live an ordinary peaceful life, and not to attempt as great an enterprise as invention. He thought of Michiko. It might be that though the old geisha pretended from her impeccable height that she did not notice anything between the two young people, in reality she might have worked out a plan for Yuki to eventually marry Michiko and take care of her in her old age. No, that was impossible. It was not possible to assume that Kosono, who was of such lofty character, had been good to him only because of a petty scheme of this sort.

Michiko appeared to him as a girl whose exterior form was developed well enough but whose interior was hopelessly un-ripened. Yuki thought of an unripe chestnut, a hard shell but watery and empty inside. He found something droll about her, but felt saddened by the curiously tenacious attitude that Michiko showed him lately while, he knew, she hated and was repelled by him. Her visits to his room, instead of being sporadic, now became more regular.

Michiko came in from the back entrance. She opened a screen between the four and one-half *tatami** living room and the twelve *tatami* guestroom in which the workshop was installed, and stood upon the rail. Resting one hand on a pillar, twisting her body a little coquettishly and holding a long sleeve with the other hand, she posed as if facing a camera. She turned her face downward and then glancing up sulkily, she said, "I came."

Yuki lying down on the veranda responded, "Ho hum."

Michiko repeated her words and received the same response. She was suddenly angry. "What a lazy way of greeting people! I'll go home and never come back again!"

"You are a spoiled brat," Yuki sat up with his legs crossed. Then, as if he had noticed her for the first time, "Well, you have a traditional hairdo today."

*One *tatami* mat (approximately 3′ x 6′) is the standard unit of floor measure for Japanese rooms.

"So what?" Michiko turned around making a twisted line with the back seam of her *kimono*.

Yuki looked at her. The contrast between the ostentatiously exaggerated attractiveness of a white neck exposed in the shape of a reversed Mt. Fuji and the straight line of her body from the hip down which revealed a young girl of no sexual quality whatsoever gave him a strange sensation. He imagined what it would be like if this girl were to be his wife waiting on him, depending upon him helplessly, yet persistently. This fancy of a would-be future without much freedom or grandeur depressed him, yet it also attracted him because of its very unpredictability. Yuki wanted to find some irresistible charm in her small and almost too finely featured face surrounded by the extended elaborate hairdo that made her forehead look even smaller.

"Turn around, it's quite becoming on you."

Michiko shrugged her shoulder and turning back she lightly touched her breast and hair in a gesture of tidying herself. "You are such a bother, really...does this satisfy you?" Flattered by Yuki's interest, with her hair ornament twinkling, she said. "I brought you something good to eat. Can you guess what it is?"

Yuki was mortified at his own weakness that invited a challenge from a mere girl. "I'm too lazy to guess. If you brought it for me, why don't you give it to me?"

Michiko immediately resented his high-handedness. "It is only out of kindness that I brought it for you. If you want to be so pompous, I am not going to give it to you." And she turned aside.

"Give it to me! I tell you, give it to me!" Yuki stood up. He was astounded at what he was going to do but could not help himself. He walked slowly over to Michiko, his body stiff like a person of absolute authority. For the first time in his life he felt an unspeakable tension within himself: the tension between the danger of entrapment and his own desperation pushing him helplessly toward it. His forehead was wet with cold sweat.

Michiko was watching him with contempt thinking that he was only joking; then it suddenly dawned upon her that something was wrong with him and she was frightened. Backing toward the living room she murmured, "No, I won't give it to you, no, never!"

Yuki was looking straight into her eyes. Their eyes met so intensely that flames could have broken out from the mere contact of their sight. He thrust his hands one after the other out of his sleeves and pressed them down on her shoulders. Now she was afraid of him. She let out a small cry, twice, then suddenly her features began to loosen, stripped of all their pretentious coyness.

"Give it to me, right now!"

The words meant nothing. She felt only the thick shivers of Yuki's strong arms, and she saw his throat move as he swallowed sour spittle.

Michiko cried, "Forgive me," with her eyes wildly open, but Yuki, as if electrified, looked pale and idiotic, fixed his stare on her, and kept sending violent shivers through her.

Michiko at last understood something in Yuki. She remembered her foster mother mentioned often that men are cowards. Here is a man, she thought, mature and self-sufficient, yet he is fighting with his cowardice over a thing like this. She wanted to pet him as if he were a big, good-natured cow. She regained control over herself and re-arranged the loosened features once more into a pretty, seductive smile.

"You silly thing, you don't have to do this, I was going to give it to you anyway," she wiped the cold sweat from Yuki's forehead. "Come this way, will you?" She took his firm arm into hers and paused an instant to listen to the wind that went through the blue foliage of the garden.

One evening when a misty May rain was falling, the old geisha came into the garden through a little gate made of twigs; she was holding an umbrella. Her *kimono* was formal with subdued color. She let the long train fall on the *tatami* and sat down.

"I dropped in on my way to work because I wanted to talk with you." Taking out the tobacco case she drew an ashtray toward her.

"I know my daughter comes here quite often. Don't misunderstand me, I have nothing against it, but, since both of you are still young, something just might happen." And about the "something," she said that if the two young people were really in love, then nothing could make her happier. "But," she continued, "if you happen to have a vague feeling like love, or a fraction of what you think is love, toward each other...well, then, there are a number of such cases in life. I myself have gone through it many times, you may encounter this sort of thing forever to no good end." Whether it be work or the love between a man and a woman, she wanted to see a person really put his entire self into it, to work on it in the most sincere and purest manner. She didn't want to die before she saw that happen to someone. "Don't hurry, don't be impatient, I want you to strike the right target, whether it is work or love. And once you find it, don't let it go."

"I don't think it is possible, these things you talk about, so pure and sincere, they just don't exist in this age." Yuki laughed heartily.

The old geisha laughed too. "In any age you would have to try very hard to make it happen. So, take as much time as you need and eat *mugitoro* to your heart's content, if you like, but try, please try to find the direction of your destiny. You are lucky enough to have a strong body, maybe you have enough energy to go on for a long time yet."

A carriage came and the old geisha went out.

Yuki left his house that night and went on a trip with no apparent purpose. He began to understand what the old geisha wanted from him: "She is trying to let me accomplish what she could not. But what she is trying to do is perhaps impossible. It is impossible either for her or for me, or even for the luckiest person, as long as he is one of us. The reality in which we are living gives us only bits and pieces now and then, but never the whole, which always flickers in front of our eyes just to tempt us, so that we still keep going on. I can reason it out for myself and give way to my limitations, but she cannot. She knows no resignation whatsoever. I pity her for that, but in a sense, this woman I pity can be much stronger than I am. What an old woman she is!" Yuki was amazed. She appears to be turning into a monster after so many years of living!

He felt sorry for the geisha, for she had an immensely tragic aspiration; but at the same time he found himself disturbed because he was trapped and carried away with this reckless scheme of hers. He wanted, if he could, to get away from the ever-ascending escalator on which the old geisha intended to put him. He wanted to cuddle up to a life like a thick and comfortable homemade feather bed.

Wishing to find an answer to these indecisive thoughts, he came to an inn by the sea about a two-hour train ride from Tokyo. The inn was run by Makita's brother and Yuki had been here before on a repair job. Here were the wide sea and the steep mountains where clouds incessantly came and went. It had never occurred to him to come and stay in a quiet place surrounded by nature such as this in order to sort out his thoughts. He was healthy, he enjoyed eating the fresh fish out of the sea, and bathing delighted him immensely.

But occasionally a roar of laughter came boiling up from inside, and he could not suppress it. It was indeed comic first of all, that the old geisha, who carried within herself such an unlimited aspiration, did not realize her real inner depth and was occupied merely by everyday trivial chores. Secondly, it was funny that he could not escape from her atmosphere, even now, miles away from her, just as a certain kind of animal cannot go beyond an enclosing line drawn on the ground. While being confined within her reach, he felt oppressed and bored, but once freed from it, he felt only loneliness. So he chose this place, thinking that he could be easily located here—and this was humorous. The relationship with Michiko was also strange and comic. Without realizing what was happening, they touched each other momentarily that one afternoon like a flash of lightning.

A week passed. Makita, the owner of the electric shop, came with money to bring him back home. Makita said, "I sympathize with you. As you are dependent, I imagine you have to put up with things you don't appreciate. My advice to you is to find a way of securing income and be independent as soon as you can."

Yuki went back with Makita, but after this he often took flight.

"Mother, Yuki escaped again, did you know?" Michiko in her tennis clothes stood at the entrance of the house. She seemed to receive a sardonic pleasure in watching her foster mother's emotional disturbance and pretended nonchalance.

"They say he didn't come home last night, or the night before."

The old geisha, who was still repeating her lessons of new Japanese music in her small, orderly private studio, put down her *shamisen*. Concealing dexterously her accumulating inward anxiety, she looked up at Michiko with her indifferent expression. "That man gave in to his bad habit again, didn't he?" She lit her long pipe and pulled her sleeve with her left hand as if to see whether her *oshima** kimono of masculine stripes looked all right.

"Never mind. I cannot give in to him all the time." And dusting off the ashes from her knees, she leisurely began to fold her music.

Disappointed by the lack of anger in her mother, Michiko, racket in hand, went out to a nearby tennis court.

*Silk dyed in mud.

As soon as the daughter had gone, however, the old geisha hurried to telephone Makita to ask him again to locate Yuki. The receiver shook violently in her hand. Her voice vibrated furiously accusing the young man she was helping of selfishness and lack of responsibility. But inside, her mind was torn by loneliness born of the ferment of her fears.

Away from the telephone, she thought to herself: That young man has a lot of spirit in him. "Well, why shouldn't he?" she murmured and touched her eyes with the tip of her sleeve. She respected him a little more each time he went away, but at the same time she could not help suffering from a sense of tremendous loss—something irreplaceable, lost forever.

In midsummer, I received some *waka* poems from Kosono who had been taking *haiku* lessons for some time. It was after dinner, and I happened to be enjoying the cool air of evening on the veranda facing the garden where the pond and the fountain were installed as gifts from the old geisha.

I unfolded the manuscript brought by a servant and listening to the sound of the water fountain, read Kosono's *waka* with much interest. I would like to introduce here one of them which I think speaks for the old geisha's recent state of mind. I have altered it a little, not as a teacher's duty but to help the reader understand. It is only a technical change, and I assure you that the original meaning is not in the least changed.

> *Year after year*
> *Sadness deepens in me,*
> *And my life flourishes*
> *Ever more.*   (1939)

NORTH COUNTRY
(Michinoku)

I T WAS THE TIME when *paulownias* were in bloom. I was walking close to the Main Street of S-Town in the Northern District. The town was the site of a castle where feudal lords had ruled for hundreds of years.

I was with several prominent members of the community. We had just left a Buddhist Temple where a spacious interior hall had been used for my lecture.

We left the temple gate and were walking along the street by a river well known for its scenic beauty. They wanted to show me the ruins of the castle on the top of the mountain. The whole mountain was enveloped with profuse green foliage, and during the day cuckoos were said to be heard in the woods.

After the lecture, I was still in a state of excitement. My mind was stirred up and I wanted to keep talking, but at the same time, I was glad my lecture was over.

The low, two-storied houses with wide overhangs were dark

and rather unevenly built along the street. Overhead was the deep blue sky of the north. In one of the houses a white heap of silkworm cocoons could be seen through the window.

"They are collecting spring cocoons," explained one of my hosts. The smell of snow-peas cooking drifted from a nearby house.

There was a barbershop with an old-fashioned sign post of red and white. By the shop was a weeping willow with its voluptuous branches almost touching the earth.

Several houses down from the willow tree, I spotted a dilapidated pseudo-western style house. It was a photo studio. A showcase with a narrow ornamental roof was attached to the front wall. I stopped to look in. I was curious, as I always am, traveling through strange provinces, to see what type of women were considered beauties and what clothes they wore. I found a picture of a lady, apparently of the upper class, who did her best to imitate Tokyo style clothing. There was one of an elderly gentleman who seemed very proud of his beard; a geisha in a curious western costume; the stiff pose of a newly-wed couple; two school girls with their hands locked together. I could not help noticing that all of the women had large, black, clear eyes. These beautiful eyes must be the distinctive trait of the people of this region.

After glancing through these pictures, my attention was drawn to a rather large picture of a young boy. It was in the center of the showcase and other photos were posted around it. It looked old and perhaps had been in the case ever since it had been taken many years ago. Maybe that is why the picture looked a little strange. But...there was something else, something strange about the boy himself, particularly about his round, generous face. And that strangeness appealed to my feelings, though I could not explain why.

The boy was wearing an expensive-looking kimono. But his beautifully-featured face had a look of such nonchalance that I wondered how the photographer could capture such a natural portrait. As far as the boy was concerned the camera did not exist. My face almost touched the glass of the case as I stared at the picture of the boy.

Seeing what had aroused my interest, one of the people in the group came and stood beside me.

"This is a picture of Shiro-Fool who was rather famous in this area."

Surprised, I repeated his words, "Did you say fool? Was he a fool then, an idiot?"

"Yes, he was an idiot, but was no ordinary fool. He was very much liked and well treated by the community."

And they told me the story of this boy, thinking perhaps the story would amuse me.

It must have been before the railways were nationalized, because the train conductors and attendants were said to have given him a ride whenever he wanted. It must have been about the turn of the century when private railroad companies were more generous and kind to the passengers.

One day, a boy clad in shabby clothes came to town. He stopped in front of a shop, took a broom from the corner and began sweeping the front yard. If it was dry and dusty, he would also take care to water the yard. When finished, he put away the broom and the pail, and stood quietly, facing the shop, with a gentle smile on his face. He looked as though he was waiting for something.

Shopkeepers did not know what he wanted at first. They scolded him and chased him away. The boy went away then, looking very sad and pitiful. Sometimes a thoughtless servant beat him, and he ran away crying and wailing.

But very soon the boy had forgotten these miserable experiences and began to smile again. Like a flowing river that could not keep debris on its surface, sadness and misery could not stay on his face long. A fresh, bright smile kept reappearing. Soon after he ran away from one shop, he was seen again sweeping the front yard of another store.

"Could he be begging for food when he finishes sweeping and stands there? That must be it."

People began to understand him.

"It's true, he is begging, but what a gentle, nice way to beg!"

One day a shopkeeper led him to the kitchen, sat him down at the table and served whatever food he could spare at the moment. The boy's face beamed.

"Yes, this is what I wanted. Why didn't you understand this before?" the boy seemed to be saying as he took *hashi* and began to eat, happy and delighted. There was nothing debasing about his attitude. His manners were both polite and refined. After eating to his heart's content, he thanked the shopkeeper: "Thank you very much for the delicious meal."

He always remembered to thank them after the meals. When people were too busy with customers, they tried to give him prepared food, rice-balls and such things, wrapped in a piece of paper, rather than taking him to the kitchen and serving him at the table. He would not accept food like that and walked away hungry, appearing almost in pain. His labor was lost and he began sweeping again for another store. It did not seem to be a real meal for him unless he could sit at a table.

He did not accept money. The few times he did take money, he lost it before he could spend it.

People talked about him.

"He must have been born in a good family."

"That explains his good manners, his politeness."

He said his name was Shiro, but he did not remember his family name. They started calling him "Shiro-Fool," but some called him "Dear Shiro-Fool" with an endearing tone in their voices. A rumor among the merchants began, "Once shops are visited by Dear Shiro-Fool, they will do well."

Having explored most of the old castle-town where he first appeared, he took off one day and went to a newly-developed city fifteen miles away. Someone must have offered him a ride.

After this experience, the boy learned to use trains and carriages. He began to wander from town to town and found that he liked travel. He could ride on anything free of charge. He went to the northernmost part of the island and even south to the Japan Sea.

He did the same thing in every town he visited; he swept the storefronts and was given meals. It was true there were misunderstandings and troubles in the beginning, but soon his innocence and gentleness captured people's minds.

"The shops Dear Shiro-Fool visits seem to do well." This was superstitious, of course, but at the same time, there was a grain of truth in it. And Shiro's visits became one of the necessities shop owners had to experience. The naive, innocent face of the boy, and his unjaundiced behavior, like that of a wandering monk, had a secret that triggered one's feelings, shifted the mood of the moment, and brought into daily life a lively and vivacious intensity.

People, especially merchants, began to welcome the boy's visit. Some shop owners went so far as to change their clothes for him. Seeing Shiro approach the shop, they put on a formal black kimono and bowed to him. Then they led him into the shop as if to welcome a god of good fortune. Cheerful processions were organized to accompany him to the station. Shiro no longer wore shabby clothes. Merchants now made him clothes of silk and satin. One big-town politician with money and power said, "It is good to bring that fool to the town. Business seems to prosper with him around."

F-Town is located at the north end of Japan. In the main street of this town, a kimono merchant had a store. The store building itself was not large, but it had a history of several generations and had a reputation of being well managed. The owner of the store had a young daughter called Ran. Shiro was very fond of the girl, and whenever he came to F-Town, he swept the front yard of her father's store. After the work was done, he came to see Ran in her living quarters. He seemed to be happy and contented just sitting with Ran. When Ran sewed, he sat there relaxed, occasionally asking simple childlike questions and amusing himself with easy games. When the sun shone into the room he would fall asleep in the caressing warm light. He would wake up once or twice, see Ran still there, feel at ease and go back to sleep again.

Ran took pity on Shiro. In spite of his unpretentious and innocent life-style, Ran could see he was afraid of the worldly activities of the people around him. But he trusted Ran completely; with her, he was secure and happy. Ran took care of him, tending his needs, like a sister or a mother.

One day, when they were sitting quietly together, she asked him, "What will you do when I get married and go away?"

Immediately the answer came, "I am coming with you."

Ran laughed, "That's impossible, Shiro. How can I take you with me when I go away to marry?"

Shiro did not understand. "But why can't I come with you?"

"Because when I am married, I will become part of my husband's family and I will have to do what they say. So, unless they say, 'Yes, you can bring Shiro with you,' I can't, you see. And I doubt if they will ever say yes."

"Are you saying you will someday belong to somebody else?"

"That's right."

"I see..."

Shiro could understand that. He understood that if Ran married someone else, she would be forever lost to him. He would be left alone, lonely and isolated in this hostile world. He understood it only too well. He could see an enemy towering over him and threatening to snatch Ran away. He became very frightened.

"You cannot marry, Miss Ran, you should never marry!"

"But I have to. Sooner or later every girl gets married."

Shiro was quiet for some time. He was thinking very hard about something. Then he struck his knee with his palm—the gesture was sheer imitation of the adults around him. And he said, "I know what I'll do—I'll marry you myself."

Ran was flabbergasted for a moment, but then she answered, "Well, I think that is a great idea!"

"Yes, sure, I'll marry you." Shiro looked very self-assured.

"If you are really going to marry me, Shiro, I want you to be a wise man, a good man. You know that, don't you?"

Ran said this without much thought, perhaps to encourage him in the difficult life he could have ahead of him.

Shiro never forgot these words of Ran's. Even though his mind was that of an eight year old (he was then around sixteen), he must have understood what marriage was.

The summer was maturing even in this northern country. But the heat was not so unbearable in F-Town, nestled in the mountain's breast, because the wind always blew from the south to the northern sea, sweeping along the streets of the town. Beyond the gentle slope, Mount-Y, which was famous for its folksongs, stood aloof and, at the foot of the mountain, waves of the summer sea glistened now and then through thin mist. There was the smell of sun-dried wheat in the air.

Ran was taking off the basting thread of a new coat she had

just finished sewing. She was sitting on the terrace. Occasionally she took her eyes from her work to admire the view of the mountain and the sea. Suddenly she heard loud voices shouting and cheering in the street. They came closer and seemed to stop in front of her father's store. Soon Shiro came into the room. Ran pretended she did not notice him. It was their little game. When he came in, he usually did not say a word and stood there quietly expecting Ran to see him first. It was the only way he knew to demand Ran's attention and perhaps her love. Ran knew this, but she liked to tease him by pretending she did not know he was there.

So Ran kept her eyes downcast for a while and then looked up, as if in surprise.

"But what happened to you, Shiro!" she cried out, genuinely surprised. "Why are you wearing those funny clothes?"

He was wearing a bright red *haori* coat and a big pointed cloth hat in matching red that hung down to the back of his head.

"I said I didn't want to, but they forced me to wear these."

Shiro was almost in tears. Ran was shaking with rage. "Take them off at once!"

With trembling hands Ran helped Shiro take off the ridiculous costume. "They go too far in making fun of you. They cannot do that. It doesn't matter if you are an idiot or not!"

Shiro repeated Ran's words. "They go too far in making fun of you. . . it doesn't matter if you are an idiot or not."

Shiro always did this. Whatever Ran said, he repeated. Ran's words were words of wisdom for him. Ran used to find this amusing and funny, but today it only made her very sad.

She brought him a cold towel and made him wipe his sweaty face. Then she gave him chilled bracken-starch pastry topped with sugar. Shiro soon got over his fear and quieted down. Sitting close to Ran, he opened up a picture book for which Ran provided explanations, who now and then took her eyes from her sewing.

"What is this?" Shiro asked pointing to a picture in the book.

"It's a railway coach."

"What is this, then?"

"A businessman, I guess. You see, he wears western clothes, and he is carrying a briefcase."

Shiro stared at the figure for a long time, and then he said, "I am going to wear western clothes myself, very soon."

Ran thought he was only imagining things. "Oh, really? That's very nice."

Shiro continued as if he was proud of it. "I'll wear western clothes and I'll sing and dance, too."

"What are you talking about, Shiro? Where would you sing? Why would you wear western clothes? Why would you do this?"

"I'll sing and dance, and I'll be a wise man, then I'll be worthy to marry you."

Ran remembered. Yes, she had heard someone mention that a promoter saw a way to profit from the popularity of Shiro-Fool and was trying to book him into a vaudeville theater. If that was the case, Ran thought, this was no joke, this was serious. Ran became frightened at the image of Shiro performing in a ridiculous vaudeville show.

"No Shiro, you must not do this. No, don't you see, this is not the way to marry me."

But Shiro was not his usual self. He would not listen to Ran. He would not let her persuade him. "Yes I will, because I must be a really wise and great man to marry you." Shiro stood up and left. Some greedy promoter must have put it in his mind that to become Ran's husband, he had no other choice but to sing and dance in vaudeville.

Soon after that Shiro disappeared from F-Town. A rumor reached Ran that an idiot clad in a uniform of gold chains did some entertainment between circus shows and sold old coins or yellow wallet ornaments with one kind of portrait or another, trinkets that were supposed to bring you good luck.

Ran knew the idiot was Shiro. She was sad and very disturbed. She could not bear to have him doing this. She tried to talk her father into bringing him back to their town. Her mother had died long ago, and Ran did not have anyone else to talk to. But her father, being a practical man of common sense, dismissed Ran's concern by saying: "No use meddling in other people's affairs... and anyway, he is an idiot."

Winter came and went; it was spring again. Ran heard that Shiro's popularity had declined and the circus abandoned him. He was now with a small company that put on vulgar shows for country folk. Wearing heavy makeup and being mocked and jeered at by the other players, he performed as a clown in slapstick comedies.

Ran felt a great pain as if her whole body was being slashed and abused. She wanted to save Shiro from the trap he was in, but there was nothing she could do. It was only a rumor she had heard; she did not know where he was. Even if he came back to

her town, she could not cure his idiocy. All the same, she wished
he had remained with her. Ran prayed to the Shinto gods and to
Buddha for Shiro's return.

Many years went by and Ran no longer heard about the idiot.
Her father died and Ran, being the only daughter had to take over
the store. Before he died, her father wanted Ran to marry so that
she would not be left alone. All her relatives wanted her to marry,
and they did their best to persuade her. But Ran refused. Coming
from an otherwise obedient and quiet daughter, this stern refusal
surprised them.

"How it would disappoint him, if Shiro should hear that I am
married," Ran thought. She wanted to spare him. Ran knew this
did not make much sense. How could he still expect to marry her?
He might not even remember her. After all, he was only a
fool. . . . But this fool somehow touched and captured her heart,
though when and how, she did not know. She could not help
herself. If she had married and lived an ordinary life, Shiro, in
some lonely and desolate corner of the world, would have been
crushed. It was only a feeling she had, but she pitied him all the
same. She would not allow herself to have this emotion, to feel
that she was responsible for his miserable fate.

One day, when the north sea roared in anger, Ran heard that
Shiro was now in Hokkaido, the northernmost island, and was
driven to doing hard chores for the company. By that time Ran
was long past the marriageable age and had given up the idea of
getting married. She had also resigned herself to the fact that she
would never see Shiro again. As far as she was concerned, Shiro
was the same as dead.

The story moved me so much that I wanted to know more about
it. So for the few days I stayed there, whenever I saw old women, I
asked if they remembered Ran and Shiro. One lady I met at my
welcome party told me, "Miss Ran is still alive, I hear. She is still
in F-Town. Since you are giving a lecture in the town, why don't
you go and visit her? She will be pleased to see you."

I did not have to look her up. When I arrived at F-Town, Ran
was there among the ladies who came to the railway station to
meet me. She had grey hair and her body was slightly bent
forward. She seemed to have some hearing difficulties. But she
carried herself very well, elegant and refined. My expectation of a
lonely, tragic figure was completely wrong. She was cheerful and
had a wonderful sense of humor, which made her both popular
and distinct among these old ladies.

We drove along the winding road up to the center of the town.
Houses were built only on one side of the street; the other side
faced the river where frogs made their songs. Ran was one of the
three ladies who rode with me in a car. As we drove up the hill,
the mountains trailed off on the left, and beyond the foot of
Mount-Y we could see the bright white caps of the sea.

I wanted to ask Ran about Shiro, but hesitated while other
people were with us. Then finding her so unpretentious and
broad-minded, I ventured to mention Shiro's name. She caught
the name immediately, and said, "Once I gave Shiro up for dead.
But lately I have changed my mind. You see, after all, he is several

years younger than I am, and since I am alive, it is possible that he is still alive. If he ever comes back, I will welcome him in my house, make him comfortable and take care of him for the rest of his life. After making up my mind to do this, I felt so much better, really relieved. I threw away his spirit tablet, which had been made at my request and kept in my family alter, and now I am trying my best to locate him. I hope someday to find him."

I watched her face with fascination. A pale white ray of hope, almost like a shadow, played across the face of the old woman who had gone through such a strange interplay of human emotions. I thought of the idiot boy whose simple and straightforward passion made so deep an impact on the woman's heart.

I was resting after dinner in a room provided for me by a rich family of the town when I was told that a guest had come to see me. It was Ran.

We talked a long while, and when our voices finally trailed off in the silence of the night, I found myself wishing Ran's wishes, and feeling her feelings. I felt I could wait for Shiro to come back, I could still wait, I could be here forever waiting for him. . . .

The lights of the squid-fishing boats began to show on the darkening sea.

(1938)

CAPRA BACK-TO-BACK SERIES

ANAIS NIN

The White Blackbird
AND OTHER WRITINGS

CAPRA PRESS
1985

Gratitude to the National Endowment for the Arts
for their valuable assistance.

Library of Congress Cataloging in Publication Data
Main entry under title:
THE WHITE BLACKBIRD (The Capra back-to-back series)
I. Nin, Anaïs, 1903-1977. White blackbird. 1985.
II. Okamoto, Kanoko, 1889-1939. Rogi sho. English. 1985.
PS3527.I865W46   1985   813'.52   84-21465
ISBN 0-88496-229-6 (pbk.)

PUBLISHED BY
CAPRA PRESS
Post Office Box 2068
Santa Barbara, CA 93120

CONTENTS

FOREWORD

After the publication of the Diaries in 1966, Anaïs Nin's circle expanded enormously. Often persons she corresponded with or met during lectures or readings, asked if they could study writing with her. She was intrigued with the idea of teaching, but in those years editing the Diaries and lecturing absorbed all her time and energy.

In 1973 International College asked Anaïs and Lawrence Durrell to take a few writing students. Based in Los Angeles but with teachers all over the world, International College was a "university without walls" which used the old guild system of a master teacher working with each student on a "one to one" basis. Anaïs wrote for their catalogue: "My methods of inspiring writers are summarized in The Novel of the Future. *It means studying all the ways of revivifying writing and reuniting it with the rhythm of life itself. It means giving a voice once again to the deep sources of metaphysical and numinous qualities contained in human*

beings and inhibited by our cultures. I think of writing as the ultimate instrument for explorations of new forms of consciousness, as a means to ecstasy, to a wider range of experience, to a deep way of communicating with other human beings. That is why I wish to teach both diary writing, which keeps us in close contact with the personal, and fiction writing, which is the expansion of what we have learned and experienced into myth and poem."

Anaïs was an excellent teacher. She was particularly good at dissolving writing blocks. To combat the inner censor, she encouraged her students to put their innermost feelings into journals which no one else would read. She sought for them the uninterrupted flow from emotion to pen that she achieved through the discipline of writing her thoughts and feelings in her diary every day from age eleven to the end of her life.

In 1974 illness forced Anaïs to discontinue her individual students. But there was such interest at International College in Nin herself as well as her teaching methods that an arrangement was made for about fifteen students to work once a week with Jody Hoy or Tristine Rainer (two of Anaïs's "daughters"—both Ph.D.s) and once a month to come to Anaïs's home in Los Angeles. The arrangement worked wonderfully for both Anaïs and her students. Anaïs always rose to the occasion seeming to find new energy. Occasionally she would insist on continuing the "one to one" relationship, talking privately with each student.

International College planned a celebration of Anaïs to be attended by the other two musketeers, Henry Miller and Lawrence

Durrell. But with Anaïs's and Henry's illness and Larry's remoteness in the South of France, it was never possible.

On January 14, 1977, Anaïs received her promotion to a higher realm.

I suggested to International College that we hold the long planned tribute on Anaïs's birthday, February 21. They agreed and rented the Scottish Rites Auditorium on Wilshire Boulevard in downtown Los Angeles. Eighteen hundred persons attended, all of whom had to write International College for tickets. Christopher Isherwood was master of ceremonies; Stephen Spender, James Leo Herlihy, Robert Kirsch, Dory Previn and others contributed. Many of Anaïs's students read works they had composed for the occasion.

Lawrence Durrell could not come from France but sent me a letter to read.

Henry Miller had hoped to come but had just suffered a serious fall on his bad leg and could not leave his home. I called him to see if he could write something for me to read. Henry remembered a preface he had written for a photobook of Anaïs that was never published. He rewrote it as a tribute. For the title he chose Venus Anadyomene—*Venus rising from the sea (foam)—a symbol Anaïs would have loved.*

—RUPERT POLE

THE WHITE BLACKBIRD

CONFINED BY THE STRAITJACKET, he smiled with a puzzled expression and looked down at his crossed arms and paralyzed legs. He was still completely out of breath from the struggle to escape from the white-coated men who held him. He himself was wearing the white coat and white hat of a chef.

Looking at him ironically, the doctor asked, "Why are you so angry? Why are you struggling so hard? What are you afraid of?"

The cook hesitated.

"Well! It's because you had everything ready to deprive me of my strength. The white blackbird is born only once every hundred years and is on the side of Good. The man in the white tie who warned me of the risk I was running belonged to the Order of the White Blackbirds, those who are born every hundred years and are on the side of Good. The white blackbird entered into me and that is why the haddock are pursuing me. They are on the side of Evil

and they have it in for me. There are six of them and sometimes they drive by in a carriage—that is, they used to drive by in a carriage, as in the etching I saw. Of course, today they drive a car and they chase me to deprive me of my strength. The president died today or else I wouldn't be here."

"But the president is not dead."

"Perhaps not, but then it was someone else who looks just like him. There is always someone who looks just like us, who thinks the same as we do, like the girl who thinks like me, the fiancee that I lost."

"Does your fiancee know you are here?"

"Not yet, but she certainly will know, since she thinks like me and the same things happen to her. That's why I am being pursued by the men and the castrated priest who sometimes appears in the form of a woman."

"Where did you see the priest?"

"Why, in the mirror! He pretends to be a woman, but he is a priest they castrated, just as you wanted to castrate me a while ago because I wanted the girl who thinks like me. Because there are more haddocks than white blackbirds and they are black and jealous. And those who are on the side of Good are always persecuted by six men dressed in gray who drive by in a carriage— or, if you prefer, in an automobile, since that is the custom nowadays."

"How do you recognize the white blackbird?"

"By its thoughts."

"You have tried to kill yourself, haven't you?"

"Yes, because nobody loves me. I was sent down to live the life

of the poet Alfred de Musset, who suffered a great deal, as you know, because nobody loved him. I was sent to live Musset's life and to explain what he prophesied before he hanged himself."

"Ah! Musset hanged himself?"

"Of course, but no one knows it and I have been sent to defend his honor."

"How are you going to defend his honor?"

"By explaining the prophecy that he uttered in a cafe just before closing time, when he stood in front of the mirror waving a towel as the Angelus rang."

"Why the Angelus?"

"Because I was born while the Angelus was ringing."

He smiled delicately. "I know very well you don't believe what I am telling you. You think I read all this in a mystery story. It's true, I've read a thousand novels because I bore the bruises of love. That girl who was my exact counterpart didn't love me, and I threw myself into the Nile, in Egypt. She always wanted to know the source of my strength, which came from the white blackbird who entered into me and which you want to take away. When one is white, one always has enemies, and I have many. There are many more haddocks than white blackbirds."

The doctor turned to me. "You see, he's incoherent. It doesn't make sense, it isn't logical. It's a clearly defined case of schizophrenia, with disassociation of the ideas. He has a persecution complex."

The cook laughed softly.

"That's funny, isn't it! But that's how it is. And I am not telling you a mystery story."

The two aides, who watched over him so that he wouldn't become dangerous, knew that he couldn't take a single step without falling down. When the doctor told him that he might go, they let him stand up and take two steps toward the door, while the doctor looked on, smiling. They let him take two steps and fall down. The doctor was allowed to continue smiling, proud of his own logic; the madman was allowed to fall, and God allowed him to say all those things about the white blackbird. It was a little bit like the road to Calvary.

Translated from the French by Jean L. Sherman

THE LITTLE GIRL IN YELLOW

from the Early Diary of Anaïs Nin, Vol. IV

Written July 30, 1929

S ITTING ALONE at the tennis club (Cercle du Bois), drowsy after a game, I watched the children playing and saw a little girl I wanted to have—an eery child with a secret smile at thoughts of her own, running lightly to dry her hands which she had dipped in the lake.

I must be beaten, I thought sadly, for I am beginning to want to pass my life on to another. Until now I never wanted children. I called them interruptions, renunciations, knowing too well that they might be neither like Hugh nor myself, not even perhaps an extension or a development of our ideals, but a mere repetition of ordinary patterns. . .

Yet this child fascinated me. She drew me out of myself— perhaps that was the blessing. I chased after her fragile self, in yellow, red, left all my weariness far away. . . She was happy to have wet hands, she was happy because the sun was drying them, she was happy to be running. All of a sudden she stood before me,

wide-eyed, startled, her arms open, her little yellow dress fluttering. I felt a second of struggle, as if the child were demanding a kind of surrender. And though my body was sore with passion, with hunger, with pain, I smiled, and she liked my smile and ran away, and ran back and around my chair, until her mother called her back.

Jamais je me donnerais entièrement à rien... Jamais je n'echapperais à moi-même, ni par l'amour, ni par la maternité, ni par l'art. Mon "moi" est comme le Dieu des croyants faibles, qui le voient partout, toujours, et ne peuve fuire cette hantise et cette vision.*

I have desired self-perfection and greatness, a very immense conceit—and now I am crushed by the weight of my ambition. I would like to pass the burden to a child.

---

*I will never give myself entirely to anything... I will never escape from myself, neither through love, nor motherhood, nor art. My self is like the God of those of little faith, who see him everywhere, always, and cannot flee this obsession and this vision.

REALISM AND REALITY

I WANT TO CLARIFY some misunderstandings that have occasionally blocked the response to my work. They arise mostly from the fact that I write as a poet in the framework of prose and appear to claim the rights of a novelist.

I deal with characters, it is true, but the best way to approach my way of dealing with them is as one regards modern painting. I intend the greater part of my writing to be received directly through the senses, as one receives painting and music. The moment you begin to look at my writing in terms of modern painting you will be in possession of one key to its meaning and will understand why I have left out so much that you are accustomed to find in character novels.

There is a purpose and form behind my partial, impressionistic, truncated characters. The whole house, or the whole body, the entire environment, may not be there, but we know from modern painting that a column can signify more than a whole house, and

that one eye can convey more than two at times. We know that in Brancusi's sculpture he achieved the closest expression of the flight of a bird by eliminating the wings.

As my books take place in the unconscious, and hardly ever outside of it, they differ from poetry not in tone, language or rhythm, but merely by the fact that they contain both the symbol and the interpretation of the symbol. The process of distillation, of reduction to the barest essentials is voluntary because dealing with the chaotic content of the unconscious in the form of the poet is natural, but to poetize and analyze simultaneously is a process which is too elusive and swift to include much upholstery.

If the writing has a dream-like quality it is not because the dramas I present are dreams, but because they are the dramas as the unconscious lives them. I never include the concrete object or fact unless it has a symbolical role to play. As in the dream when a chair appears in my book it is because this chair has something portentious to reveal about the drama that is taking place. Thus alone can I achieve the intensification and vividness of a kind of drama which we know to be highly elusive and fragmentary and which takes place usually only in psychoanalysis.

These dramas of the unconscious to gain a form and validity of their own must temporarily displace the over-obtrusive, dense, deceptive settings of our outer world which usually serve as concealment, so that we may become as familiar with its inner properties and developments as we are with the workings of our conscious, external worlds.

As in Miro's painting, the circus is indicated by a line, a red ball, and space. This conforms to my concept that modern writing

must have the swift rhythm of our time, and be as lightly cargoed as the airplane to permit flight and speed. It is my belief that emotionally as well as scientifically, we are going to travel more lightly and that writing will not belong to our time if it does not learn to travel faster than sound!

And how are we going to fly with novels which begin: "She was sitting under a 40 Watt Mazda lamp" (the author I will not quote for fear of libel.)

The new investigations of the unconscious have brought people nearer to poetry, for every man now knows that he is continuously constructing a dream duplicate of his life in the same symbolical terms used familiarly by the poets and that he too possesses a very subtle and intricate way of dramatizing the concealed meaning of his life.

At night every man dreams in the imagery of the poets, but in the daytime he denies and rejects the world of the artist as if it were not his world, even to the length of classifying such dream activity as symptomatic of neurosis when it is actually a symptom of the creativity latent in every man.

These investigations will also make us more impatient with the opaque quality of our external world which is used in most novels as defenses against a disturbing deeper world, as an obstacle in reaching it, as an obstruction created by fear; and a greater impatience even with meaningless acts, with all evasions of the essential inner drama practiced by the so-called realistic novel in which we are actually being constantly cheated of reality and experience.

The occasional resistance I have encountered has been due, I

believe, to my use of the symbolical, my use of daily objects not as they stand around us as reassuring, consoling solidities, like a cup of coffee, or an alarm clock, but that I come like a magician of doubtful authenticity and transform this cup of coffee and this alarm clock into stage property for a story which then seems like a dream and not reality.

Yet everyone does this, as we know, every night, whenever he begins to interpret or dramatize the deeper significance of his acts.

Now I place you in a world which is like the world of the dream, sparingly furnished only with the objects which have proved their symbolical value, and not their familiar value as objects which give us our daily gravitational security. It is because I assume that the world of the dream like the world of my books is actually the way we re-experience our life, and I expect people to recognize its contours or its lack of contours without fear (the most disturbing element of the dream is that it has no frames, no walls, no doors and no boundaries...like my novels.) Whatever anxiety my writing may create can only be the anxiety people feel in the presence of an incomplete but highly significant dream.

I cannot claim the privileges granted to the poet (he is allowed his mystery and praised for what he does not reveal) because the poet is content with bringing forth the flow of images but does not set about to interpret them as characters. All mysteries become explicit when they are personified and dramatized, and I tend towards a greater explicitness, but not before the reality of the inner drama is made completely valid in itself.

The conventionalities of the novel can no longer communicate what we know. That is why James Joyce exploded the form of the

novel and let his writing erupt in a veritable flow. As Edmund Wilson put it: "Just as Joyce in *Ulysses* laid the *Odyssey* under requisition to help provide a structure for his material—a material which, once it had begun to gush forth from the rock of Joyce's sealed personality at the blow of Aaron's rod of free associations, threatened to rise and submerge the artist like the floods which the sorceress's apprentice let loose by his bedeviled broom."

But there is no need to seek a structure from the old myths. In the human unconscious itself, once unravelled, there is an indigenous structure and pattern. If we are able to detect and seize and use it we have the conflicts and the forms of the novel of the future.

The pattern of the new novel will be one in which everything will be produced only as it is discovered by the emotions: by associations and repetitions, by associative memory as in Proust, by repetitious experiences out of which the meaning finally becomes clear as it does in life, alone making it possible to seize the inner pattern and not the false exterior ones. The pattern of the deeper life covered and disguised will be uncovered and demasked by the writer's process of interpretation of the symbolical meaning of people's acts, not a mere reporting of them or of their words. The incoherence of such a way of writing, often practiced by D.H. Lawrence, is only apparent and ceases as soon as the writer strikes the deepest level of all, for the unconscious creates the most consistent patterns and plots of all.

Many novels today include the psychoanalytical experience. That is only a crude makeshift. The novelist knows that psychoanalysis has uncovered layers not uncovered in the narrative novel

(particularly in a society where people's acts no longer correspond to their inner impulses; this does not apply, for instance, to the Dostoevskian novels in which people act by the impulses of their unconscious, as we do not.) But so far he has granted this uncovering power only to the professional analyst, not realizing that this power must become an integral part of his novelist's equipment.

Historical knowledge as it was used by a Joyce or a Proust was never introduced into the novel as pure history but as an integrated part of the novelist's total vision. Thus the new perspective of character as it can be created by the novelist familiar with the unconscious will be slowly integrated within the novel and will not need to be voiced through a doctor. The novelist has allowed the doctor to do what he felt impotent to do himself, shifting the responsibilities of breaking through false patterns, disguises, thus increasing the reader's feelings that neurosis in a character made it a "case" and not an experience very common in our world today, which it is. The novelist himself has not yet accepted the unconscious activity, the unconscious dramas as an integral part of all characters.

A woman was complaining of her bad health to a friend and this friend said, "With you I'm sure it's not a neurotic complaint."

"Of course not," said the sick woman, "it's not neurotic. It's just human."

If we can accept neurosis as a part of our humanity it will cease to be a case in literature and become one of the richest sources of fiction writing.

There is no denying that we are suffering from a collective

neurosis and the novel which does not face this is not a novel of our time. Collective neurosis can no longer be dismissed as exceptional, pathological or decadent. It is a direct result of our social system. As soon as we accept this we are ready to face the causes and to reach into deeper relations to history.

While we refuse to organize the confusions within us we will never have an objective understanding of what is happening outside. We will not be able to relate to it, to choose sides, to evaluate historically and consequently we will be incapacitated for action. The novelist's preoccupation with inner distortions is not morbid or a love of illness but it comes as a truthful mirror of today's drama. In order to take action full experience is required. All novels which contribute to our emotional atrophy only deepen our blindness. The novels today do not reflect our life but people's fear of life, of experience, of the deeper layers of self knowledge by which we alone can defeat tragedy.

Reportage, the other extreme from unconscious writing, is not reality either, because facts stated objectively, scientifically, statistically without the artist's power to communicate their meaning do not give us an emotional experience. And nothing that we do not discover emotionally will have the power to alter our vision. In reportage we are once more cheated of experience, and realism is substituted for reality.

As soon as I say experience there are some who grow afraid again, who think that experience means to be first of all everything one writes about. But by experience I do not always mean to act, but to feel. A young writer said to me one day: "I saw a workman who had had his hand torn off by a machine. I didn't

feel anything." Such a person is not ony schizophrenic; he is no doubt a bad writer. To experience this one does not have to be the workman to whom this happened.

The richest source of creation is feeling, followed by a vision of its meaning. The medium of the writer is not ink and paper but his body: the sensitivity of his eyes, ears and heart. If these are atrophied let him give up writing.

THE NEW WOMAN

WHY ONE WRITES is a question I can answer easily, having so often asked it of myself. I believe one writes because one has to create a world in which one can live. I could not live in any of the worlds offered to me—the world of my parents, the world of war, the world of politics. I had to create a world of my own, like a climate, a country, an atmosphere in which I could breathe, reign, and recreate myself when destroyed by living. That I believe is the reason for every work of art.

The artist is the only one who knows that the world is a subjective creation, that there is a choice to be made, a selection of elements. It is a materialization, an incarnation of his inner world. Then he hopes to attract others into it. He hopes to impose his particular vision and share it with others. And when the second stage is not reached, the brave artist continues nevertheless. The few moments of communion with the world are worth the pain,

for it is a world for others, an inheritance for others, a gift to others in the end.

We also write to heighten our own awareness of life. We write to lure and enchant and console others. We write to serenade our lovers. We write to taste life twice, in the moment and in retrospection. We write, like Proust, to render all of it eternal, and to persuade ourselves that it is eternal. We write to be able to transcend our life, to reach beyond it. We write to teach ourselves to speak with others, to record the journey into the labyrinth. We write to expand our world when we feel strangled, or constricted, or lonely. We write as the birds sing, as the primitives dance their rituals. If you do not breathe through writing, if you do not cry out in writing, or sing in writing, then don't write, because our culture has no use for it. When I don't write, I feel my world shrinking. I feel I am in a prison. I feel I lose my fire and my color. It should be a necessity, as the sea needs to heave, and I call it breathing.

GUILT FOR CREATING

For too many centuries we have been busy being "muses" to the artists. And I know you have followed me in the diary when I wanted to be a muse, and I wanted to be the wife of the artist, but I was really trying to avoid the final issue—that I had to do the job myself. In letters I've received from women, I've found what Rank had described as a guilt for creating. It's a very strange illness, and it doesn't strike men—because the culture has demanded of man that he give his maximum talents. He is encouraged by the culture, to become the great doctor, the great philosopher, the

great professor, the great writer. Everything is really planned to push him in that direction. Now this was not asked of women. And in my family, just as in your family probably, I was expected simply to marry, to be a wife, and to raise children. But not all women are gifted for that, and sometimes, as D.H. Lawrence properly said, "We don't need more children in the world, we need hope."

So this is what I set out to do, to adopt all of you. Because Baudelaire told me a long time ago that in each one of us there is a man, a woman, and a child—and the child is always in trouble. The psychologists are always confirming what the poets have said so long ago. You know, even poor, maligned Freud said once, "Everywhere I go, I find a poet has been there before me." So the poet said we have three personalities, and one was the child fantasy which remained in the adult and which, in a way, makes the artist.

When I talk so much of the artist, I don't mean only the one who gave us music, who gave us color, who gave us architecture, who gave us philosophy, who gave us so much and enriched our life. I mean the creative spirit in all its manifestations. Even as a child, when my father and mother were quarreling—my father was a pianist and my mother was a singer—when music time came, everything became peaceful and beautiful. And as children we shared the feeling that music was a magical thing which restored harmony in the family and made life bearable for us.

Now there was a woman in France—and I give her story because it shows how we can turn and metamorphose and use everything to become creative. This was the mother of Utrillo.

Because she was very poor, the mother of Utrillo was condemned to be a laundress and a houseworker. But she lived in Montmartre at the time of almost the greatest group of painters that were ever put together, and she became a model for them. As she watched the painters paint, she learned to paint. And she became, herself, a noted painter, Suzanne Valadon. It was the same thing that happened to me when I was modelling at the age of sixteen, because I didn't have any profession and I didn't know how else to earn a living. I learned from the painters the sense of color, which was to train me in observation my whole life.

I learned many things from the artist which I would call creating out of nothing. Varda, for example, taught me that collage is made out of little bits of cloth. He even had me cut a piece of the lining of my coat because he took a liking to the color of it and wanted to incorporate it into a collage. He was making very beautiful celestial gardens and fantasies of every possible dream with just little bits of cloth and glue. Varda is also the one who taught me that if you leave a chair long enough on the beach, it becomes bleached into the most beautiful color imaginable which you could never find with paint.

I learned from Tinguely that he went to junkyards, and he picked out all kinds of bits and pieces of machines and built some machines which turned out to be caricatures of technology. He even built a machine which committed suicide, which I described in a book called *Collages*. I am trying to say that the artist is a magician—that he taught me that no matter where you were put, you can always somehow come out of that place.

Now I was placed somewhere you might imagine would be

terribly interesting, a suburb of Paris. But a suburb of Paris can be just as lonely as a suburb of New York or Los Angeles or San Francisco. I was in my twenties and I didn't know anyone at the time, so I turned to my love of writers. I wrote a book, and suddenly I found myself in a Bohemian, artistic, literary writer's world. And that was my bridge. But sometimes, when people say to me, that's fine, but you were gifted for writing, my answer is that there is not always that kind of visible skill.

I know a woman who started with nothing, whom I consider a great heroine. She had not been able to go to high school because her family was very poor and had so many children. The family lived on a farm in Saratoga, but she decided to go to New York City. She began working at Brentano's and after a little while told them that she wanted to have a bookshop of her own. They laughed at her and said that she was absolutely mad and would never survive the summer. She had $150 saved and she rented a little place that went downstairs in the theater section of New York, and everybody came in the evening after the theater. And today her bookshop is not only the most famous bookshop in New York, the Gotham Book Mart, but it is a place where everybody wants to have bookshop parties. She has visitors from all over the world—Virginia Woolf came to see her when she came to New York, Isak Dinesen, and many more. And no other bookshop in New York had that fascination which came from her, her humanity and friendliness, and the fact that people could stand there and read a book and she wouldn't even notice them. Now Francis Steloff is her name, and I mention her whenever anyone claims that it takes a particular skill to get out of a restricted,

limited or impoverished life. Francis is now eighty-six, a beautiful old lady with white hair and perfect skin who has defied age.

It was the principle of creative will that I admired and learned from musicians like Eric Satie, who defied starvation and used his compositions to protect his piano from the dampness of his little room in a suburb of Paris. Even Einstein, who disbelieved Newton's unified field theory, died believing what is being proved now. I give that as an instance of faith, and faith is what I want to talk about. What kept me writing, when for twenty years I was received by complete silence, is that faith in the necessity to be the artist—and no matter what happens even if there is no one listening.

I don't need to speak of Zelda Fitzgerald. I think all of you have thought about Zelda, how she might never have lost her mind if Fitzgerald had not forbidden her to publish her diary. It is well known that Fitzgerald said no, that it could not be published, because he would need it for his own work. This, to me, was the beginning of Zelda's disturbance. She was unable to fulfill herself as a writer, and was overpowered by the reputation of Fitzgerald. But if you read her own book, you will find that in a sense she created a much more original novel than he ever did, one more modern in its effort to use language in an original way.

History, much like the spotlight, has hit whatever it wanted to hit, and very often it missed the woman. We all know about Dylan Thomas. Very few of us know about Caitlin Thomas, who after his death wrote a book which is a poem in itself and sometimes surpasses his own—in strength, in primitive beauty, in a real wake of feeling. But she was so overwhelmed by the talent of Dylan

Thomas that she never thought anything of her writing at all until he died.

THE WOMAN OF THE FUTURE

So we're here to celebrate the sources of faith and confidence. I want to give you the secrets of the constant alchemy that we must practice to turn brass into gold, hate into love, destruction into creation—to change the crass daily news into inspiration, and despair into joy. None need misinterpret this as indifference to the state of the world or to the actions by which we can stem the destructiveness of the corrupt system. There is an acknowledgement that as human beings, we need nourishment to sustain the life of the spirit, so that we can act in the world, but I don't mean turn away. I mean we must gain our strength and our values from self-growth and self-discovery. Against all odds, against all handicaps, against the chamber of horrors we call history, man has continued to dream and to depict its opposite. That is what we have to do. We do not escape into philosophy, psychology and art—we go there to restore our shattered selves into whole ones.

The woman of the future, who is really being born today, will be a woman completely free of guilt for creating and for her self-development. She will be a woman in harmony with her own strength, not necessarily called masculine, or eccentric, or something unnatural. I imagine she will be very tranquil about her strength and her serenity, a woman who will know how to talk to children and to the men who sometimes fear her. Man has been uneasy about this self-evolution of woman, but he need not be—

because, instead of having a dependent, he will have a partner. He will have someone who will not make him feel that every day he has to go into battle against the world to support a wife and child, or a childlike wife. The woman of the future will never try to live vicariously through the man, and urge and push him to despair, to fulfill something that she should really be doing herself. So that is my first image—she is not aggressive, she is serene, she is sure, she is confident, she is able to develop her skills, she is able to ask for space for herself.

I want this quality of the sense of the person, the sense of direct contact with human beings to be preserved by woman, not as something bad, but as something that could make a totally different world where intellectual capacity would be fused with intuition and with a sense of the personal.

Now when I wrote the diary and when I wrote fiction, I was trying to say that we need both intimacy and a deep knowledge of a few human beings. We also need mythology and fiction which is a little further away, and art is always a little further away from the entirely personal world of the woman. But I want to tell you the story of Colette. When her name was suggested for the *Académie Francais*, which is considered the highest honor given to writers, there was much discussion because she hadn't written about war, she hadn't written about any large event, she had only written about love. They admired her as a writer, as a stylist—she was one of our best stylists—but somehow the personal world of Colette was not supposed to have been very important. And I think it is extremely important because it's the loss of that intimacy and the loss of that person-to-person sense which the

woman has developed, because she has been more constricted and less active in the world. So the family was very important, the neighbor was very important, and the friend was very important.

It would be nice if men could share that, too, of course. And they will, on the day they recognize the femininity in themselves, which is what Jung has been trying to tell us. I was asked once how I felt about men who cried, and I said that I loved men who cried, because it showed they had feeling. The day that woman admits what we call her masculine qualities, and man admits his so-called feminine qualities, will mean that we admit we are androgynous, that we have many personalities, many sides to fulfill. A woman can be courageous, can be adventurous, she can be all these things. And this new woman who is coming up is very inspiring, very wonderful. And I love her.

From a talk given April 1971 in San Francisco as part of a celebration of women in the arts.

PREFACE TO LIVRE IVRE

THERE ARE DEPTHS into which most human beings do not dare to descend. These are infernos of our instinctive life, the journey through our nightmares necessary to rebirth. The mythological journey of the hero includes the great battles with our demons. Marcel Moreau is engaged in this battle. At first I thought of him as the Lilauea volcano in Hawaii. Ascending toward its vast pit the trees, flowers, bushes, birds, fruit grew rarer and finally there were none at all. The soft earth had been covered by black lava, not shining as it does when wet and erupting, but the dead color of the blackest ash. It hardened. It burnt trees to bone-white skeletons. Approaching it, it smoked still, ready for other eruptions. It was a vast crater. One could walk on its rim, looking down at the infernal pit. It smelled of sulphur. There was a silence, a suspense, for everyone who leaned over knew what had come before, a wild incredible explosion, fountains of fire, rocks propelled in the air. But in the end, in Livre Ivre, one

does not experience devastation or destruction from Moreau's explosion of fire. He is in search of his humanity, and is dynamiting the obstacles and the injuries which impede his quest. He returns to his childhood. The portrait of his father is deeply moving.

"Tant de pauvres meurent sans donner l'impression d'avoir vecu."

"Sa mort a fait de moi un lutteur."

He is suspicious of woman even though:

"Je crois que d'elle seule peut venir l'absolu."

The obstacle to woman was created by the mother. We suffer his schooling, his battles. He exists *sur un pied de guerre.*

"Dans ma famille regnait une sorte de puritanisme sans Dieu."

One feels that if he did not combat he would be possessed by an unfulfillable love and tenderness. Meanwhile his hostility is a kind of passion. In his own beautiful words from a letter to me:

"It is not enough that writing should be a song, it must intoxicate, drug, it must provoke in the reader those sumptuous disturbances without which there are no deep revelations. My wish is to introduce wine in the French language, to write a book which could be danced rather than read."

It is the energy of fire which creates our world. I think of the new earth, lava at first, burning and then cooling and giving birth to the most daring flowers.

His desires are thwarted: he asks for books and is given other objects. He has to struggle not to be submerged by the mother. If his other books were like elemental storms, this one seeks the cause for his furies, his revenges.

"Ce qui m'attriste et me revolte a la fois, c'est d'avoir ete le temoin de tant de destinees closes."

Then he discovers the world of the writers.

"Je joue avec ces moments de la vie qui me firent mal, je les integre sans difficultes au chant general d'une demarche qui s'est trempee dans ses profondeurs en vue de culminer dans l'ivresse."

Ecstasy is to be won through the magic power of language. To all the selves in us which are silent, which cannot speak, Moreau gives a tongue. Because he believes that *"chaque homme se doit de devenir le monstre dont il possede en lui, ravages, mutiles, maudits, toutes les composants. En verite nous sommes un puzzle terrible ou il n'est aucune piece qui ne soit defigure our distordue par la societe. A nous de le reconstituer contre elle, en lui ajoutant les eclairs fabuleux de la nuit."*

By a series of explosions, the poet uncovers what he believes: *"que le souterrain est le royaume de la vie, le repaire de l'ivresse, le bonheur des ombres et des illuminations."*

PREFACE TO
ANTHOLOGY OF WOMEN'S POETRY

JEAN COCTEAU SAID that poetry was indispensable, but he did not know why. This anthology may answer the question, for every mood, every experience, every aspect of the world, demands expression, and here we might turn casually to any page, and find the words we need for indignation, anger, injustice, love, passion, religious and pagan prayers, cries of distress and cries of joy. We can turn to it on blank days when either our sorrows or our joys do not find their voice. So many poets are gathered here together to voice the entire range of human experience, in every variation of voice and tone, employing every color and every texture, every level of talk, from metamorphosis to plain and homely untransfigured statements.

Poetry is no longer to be defined as of old, it has opened its doors to direct statements, to slogans, to marching songs, to hymns and to street songs. It is no longer a solitary chant, it has become common to all and inclusive of all races, religions and

irreligions. The variety of levels and themes makes these poems universal. But it also focuses on revelations of women which needed to be heard. Every age is represented, every race, every individual variation, but ultimately this poetry, this anthology is the song of women.

My own definition of the poet is he who teaches us levitation, because I feel poetry is needed to lift us above despair, and above our human condition, so we may become aware that we need not be overwhelmed by the weight of earth, the ponderous oppression of quotidian burdens. The burdens here are dwelt upon, poetry in this anthology is not only the transformer or the indicator to other forms of life. It is the poetry of today, and the poetry of woman at a crucial period of evolution. The selection is wide and broad. It will place poetry as a daily necessity, as a nourishment, as useful to the community, the equivalent of our daily speech, our daily thoughts and feeling. In this way it may prove its indispensable quality. In the terms of Gaston Bachelard, the poet philosopher and philosopher of poetry, we have here the poetics of fire, space, earth, air and water.

Gaston Bachelard writes that "poetry gives us mastery of our tongue." And only by this mastery can we make ourselves understood by others, and make our needs, our demands, our predicaments, our dilemmas, known.

He also writes: "There is no need to have lived through the poet's suffering in order to seize the felicity of speech offered by the poet—a felicity that dominates tragedy itself." And: "To mount too high, or descend too low, is allowed in the case of the poet, who brings earth and sky together."

The poet helps us to see more, to hear more, to discover within ourselves such landscapes, such emotions, such reveries, such relationships to people, to nature, to experience as may remain unknown to us before they describe it, for to sustain our dreams and our lover's needs, we need to absorb from the poet his capacity for seeing and hearing what daily life obscures from us.

Two kinds of space, intimate and outer, struggle for our attention, and struggle for integration, for in integration and fusion lies the power of ecstasy which enables us to conquer despair and conquer human oppression.

Rilke said: "The plain is the sentiment which exalts us." But the description of the not plain is what sustains us in our search, the description of the marvelous states of consciousness attainable is what propels us upward rather than downward.

Poetry, no matter what its subject, can propel us forward, for it gives to man's most ordinary experience, the glow of a tale, the illumination of myth, the song's contagious rhythm, a troubadour's romance.

Gaston Bachelard again: "Any sentiment that exalts us makes our situation in the world smoother."

When history, when our world becomes intolerable, the young turn to poetry. They write enormous amounts of it, they sing it, they print it themselves. It is the creative drug, the creative painkiller, the creative tranquilizer, the creative healer.

This is an era of poetry, poetry against the inarticulate, the stuttering, the muttering wordless suffering which cannot be shared or heard. The skillful, the clarified expression of our joys and sorrows, our angers and rebellions, makes them sharable and

therefore less destructive. Words as exorcism of pain, indispensable to fraternization, the opposite of war.

The fusion here is in the voice of woman. Woman determined to end woman's mysteries and woman's secrets. We need to know her better. Let us approach here and listen to her in these condensed, in these concentrated and distilled messages, to become intimate with her.

It is not only the Oriental women who wore veils. There are psychic veils, and these are best lifted by the poet, so we can acquire from the poet at the same time his constant rediscovery of love.

PREFACE FOR HARVARD ADVOCATE

WOMEN HAVE ALWAYS been writers. It was the one profession which did not conflict with the rules imposed on her or the limitations and restrictions of her professional expansion. But this is a dazzling moment for women; it is the moment when the world has become aware of her achievements. For even as writers, women encountered prejudice or at least indifference. At one time they took names of men to be able to assert their work: Georges Sand, George Elliot. And the election of Colette to the French Academy was bitterly fought on the ground that she merely wrote about love affairs and personal entanglements.

The very restrictions and limitations gave women's writing an added dimension: writing benefited from being at times her only means of expression. She perfected it. In the year 900 a Japanese woman wrote the first chronicle of life at court, the *Tale of Gengi*, equal to a Proustian achievement in subtlety of psychology and care for detail.

40

The writing of women can bear the new intense light of recognition thrown upon it by the woman's liberation movement. It can bear revaluation and critical examination. Women like Anna Balakian and Sharon Spencer have become themselves acute and skillful critics.

The fact that woman was not always involved in larger issues of history or politics increased her vision of deeper issues, those of human values, human concerns, and the value of personal relationship to sustain our humanity endangered by technology and by politician's power drives. History is the story of man's thirst for power with its consequent inhumanity. The writing of women may indicate a new feminine direction. In Yoko Ono's words: "We can evolve rather than revolt, come together rather than claim independence and feel rather than think."

A proper evaluation, a proper perspective and appreciation of women's writing may help to balance the unbalanced forces of the world today. If we have had an excess of violence, of crime and war, we may find in women's writing the persistent devotion to opposite concerns.

WOMEN OF NEW YORK

THE CHARACTERISTIC ASPECT of the women of New York is that they are in motion, perpetually active and that one would have to photograph them at a speed used for ballet dancers or athletes. Coming from above, say in a helicopter, we see first on the twenty-fourth floor of one of the highest glass buildings facing the United Nations, Mrs. Millie Johnstone who initiated the first Japanese Tea Ceremony School in New York to counterbalance its hectic, frenzied activity. Her apartment, one of the most beautiful in New York, is decorated with some of her own tapestries evoking the Bethlehem Steel Works of her husband, with collages by Varda, wool rugs from Peru, and has a view of the Hudson which seems like a view from a transatlantic liner. One room is shuttered by a trellis of wood and frosted glass, subdued and simple. It is a Japanese room, in the style of classical Japanese austerity. A low couch, filtered light, a platform covered by a grass mat for the tea ceremony, the utensils,

42

the pot, the cups, the brush, the spoon, the napkin, the wafer. Mrs.
Johnstone dispenses the calm and serenity of the ritual in a blue
kimono. Having been a dancer she is very graceful and her New
England profile melts into the formal design expected of Oriental
stylization. She feels that modern men and women need to learn
repose and meditation to sustain themselves in a city of frenzy.

Uptown, in a private house, in an apartment which opens on a
backyard as some of the private houses still do in New York, lives
a chic, slim, attractive woman, Dr. Inge Begner. Sitting in a deep,
modern plastic black and white chair, knitting, speaking in a soft
voice, with lively, keen expression and the most outstanding
knowledge of semantics, she wields an influence over the life of
New York on two levels, which throw their cumulative power in a
widening circle difficult to measure. She treats the neurosis
spawned by the city, every day, every hour, creating a circle of
sanity, of renewed strength, for New York is like a vast computer,
ruthless to human beings. She advises young men in trouble with
their draft board, parents who do not know how to be parents,
creative people defeated by commercialism, the confused, the
discouraged, the lost.

She was born in a small town in Bavaria. Her father was a
doctor reputed for his liberalism. Her second activity is in politics,
so that her teachings, her psychological insights are not only
applied in her office, individually, but she acts out the commit-
ments they point to. Not theory but practice. She has participated

in marches, has walked the streets of her neighborhood seeking votes. She is a woman in action, in harmony with her insights.

Xavore Poue is a professional pianist practicing for a concert in a studio in New York. She is a tall and handsome woman. But she is best known as the woman who writes about astrology for *Harper's Bazaar*. The monthly horoscopes are written with imagination and poetry and even when they do not necessarily fit the person one wishes they did. It is a destiny, a life designed by an artist and preferable to reality, for its ambiguity allows for surprises.

On New Year's Eve she is the only one who practices the ritual of putting melted lead into cold water and reading the modern sculpture hieroglyphs as predictions.

She has studied minerals, herbs, health foods, and relates astrology to other knowledge. I would trust her portrait of anyone, for like the lover, she sees the potential self who might be. She is herself born in the sign of our age so should be able to read its intentions.

Now we travel to the Village, west on notorious Bleeker Street, beyond the cafes and the rock-and-roll nightclubs, where the antique shops begin, arts and crafts boutiques. We are visiting America's greatest writer, Marguerite Young. Art is the nightlife

of the people. Marguerite Young is the describer of the American subconscious, just as James Joyce was of his own race. She is totally committed to the pursuit of this oceanic unconscious nightlife. Her apartment is all in red and filled with collections of dolls, angels, tin soldiers, a circus horse, mementoes, sea shells, Indian necklaces—a children's paradise. The walls are covered with books. Already celebrated for a classic *Miss MacIntosh, My Darling*, she is modest, continues to teach, eats at drugstores, converses with anyone at all, lives most intensely within the book she is writing so that you are taken into the world she is exploring at the moment, its comic aspects, its anecdotal surprises, its associative infinities. This earthy-looking, plain spoken, middle western American, wafts you into spatial semantic games, elasticities of wildest imagination. For America who only looks at its day action face, this oceanographer of the deep is a phenomenon. When she works the pages cover all her floors, furniture, bookcases, divans, couch, chairs. One day they will fall over the city of New York outshining the paper rain for the astronauts.

In another pink house lives an even more symbolic figure of New York women, for she lives in luxury without serenity, and writes books of poems between telephone calls, hairdressers and dressmakers, frivolities, social activities. She is young and beautiful, graces the pages of *Harper's Bazaar*, is restless, whirling, hectic, paying attention only for sixty seconds, starting a hundred new lives a day, wishing to live in an orange grove in California, to be

back in Hong Kong or Cambodia, seeing everyone who has a name, dropping in on her little girl with her governess while they take air in the park, saying she cannot write poems all day, so she studies Chinese exercises and writes about them, about sea shells, is everywhere, knows everyone, never rests anywhere like a female hummingbird whose hum, the poem, she must write how and when? One does not know. When she calls up it is a cry of distress, typical of New York *bas*, for it is repetitious: New York is a poison (ambition) one cannot believe in friendship. Life is not real (in New York). I am lonely, everyone admits over the telephone, behind the gusto the glitter, the metallic surface, the glamor, the activity. The poem comes out smiling, witty. It is a sport to smile, glide, propelled by what? Who?

Written by Anaïs Nin in 1930 at the age of
twenty-seven. Taken from notes at end of
Diary Vol. 30. Not published in
The Early Diary of Anaïs Nin—Vol. 4 (1927-31).

PORTRAIT OF what I would have liked to have been.
Eternally a woman of thirty, full-breasted, tall, black
hair, Oriental-Spanish eyes and aquiline nose—very
pale—exotic looking—extremely experienced—author of five or
six books of five or six different kinds (synthetic résumé of all
interesting attitudes)—unmarried (lovers permitted)—rich enough
to help out writers and publish a magazine—a great traveller. At
thirty-one I would meet Hugh and have two children (Hugh being
the only man I would like to have children from) and sit in an old
garden like this one and be really happy.

NOTE: *Hugh was her husband and the garden was Louveciennes.*

This second volume of the
Capra Back-to-Back Series
was printed for Capra Press
by Kingsport Press in Kingsport, Tennessee,
during April 1985.
Cover design by Francine Rudesill.
Typography and design by Jim Cook
for Cook/Sundstrom Associates.

This second volume of the
Capra Back-to-Back Series
was printed for Capra Press
by Kingsport Press in Kingsport, Tennessee,
during April 1985.
Cover design by Francine Rudesill.
Typography and design by Jim Cook
for Cook/Sundstrom Associates.